The Erotic Comedies

The Vassi Collection

Volume XI

The Erotic Comedies

Marco Vassi

OPEN ROAD

INTEGRATED MEDIA

NEW YORK

This edition published in 2014 by Open Road Integrated Media, Inc.
345 Hudson Street
New York, NY 10014
www.openroadmedia.com

for bruce, dolores, evelyn,
gerard, and timothy,
for joining me in the lab

with special thanks
to betty and ted for bears in Vermont;
to john, louisa, albert, and bruce
for their loving care in converting
three of the fables into wondrous theatre;
to al, jack, lige, and gay
for courage in publishing
what others were afraid to touch;
and to richard
for keeping the faith

and an astral toast
to the ghost of james fenimore cooper
who haunts the steam room
at the st. mark's baths

Acknowledgments

To the following publications, for permission to reprint pieces which first appeared in their pages: *Penthouse*, Circus of Jade, Thy Kingdom of Come, The Metasexual Manifesto; *Oui*, The Dying Gynecologist, Bluebeard's Instant Grecian Urn, Subway Dick; *Gallery*, Yesterday's Iago; *Gay*, The Trucks; *Screw*, Beyond Bisexuality; Bisexuality, Therapy, and Revolution.

Contents

Introduction

Martin Shepard, M.D.

I first met Marco Vassi in a somewhat fashionable Chinese restaurant on Manhattan's upper west side in the fall of 1968. It was evening, and a mutual friend had decided to introduce us. It was a case of love at first sight. No. Take that back. It was a case of intrigue at first sight.

What I saw was a slim, swarthy man in his early thirties, of moderate height, unshaven, full sensual lips posed in a mischievous smile, and a sense of great anguish pouring from dark, deep-set eyes. His costume for the evening? Oversized, stained, grey overalls. He looked like a cross between an Italian street urchin and a young Karl Marx.

Love grew as soon as he began to speak. It was as if I discovered the brother I had always sought, a man whose curiosities, playfulness, reflections on mortality, and sexual hungers mirrored my own. Nothing that he said or did seemed accidental, and I left that encounter realizing that even his stained dress was purposeful. If there was *schmutz*, it was holy *schmutz*, for he was trying to understand his natural response to dirt free of cultural conditioning.

We saw one another frequently over the next two years. Outfront and outrageous, Marco had a way of posing questions to which he knew there were no answers. As a Zen Buddhist, his deepest aspiration was enlightenment. As an ex-Catholic, his way of attaining it was through sexual yoga. With raw courage sustained by the most tenuous conviction that sex is smiled upon by the Atman, he plunged into the world of eroticism. In the words of one of his characters (laying gender prejudice aside), "it was impossible for her to remember how many men, women, children, animals and dildoes had been inside her, how many gallons of sperm she had swallowed, which perverse actions she had not attempted or catered to."

We met infrequently during the next several years. Other commitments, other adventures, and other friendships occupied both of us. I would, on occasion, pick up a national magazine that contained an article of his or purchase some new soft cover title. It amazed me that given his prolific output and his enormous literary talent, critical acclaim seemed to avoid him. He was certainly the best erotic writer I had ever read. Perhaps that was the problem, for neither The New York Times Book Review nor any other major reviewer seemed to acknowledge the presence of this class of literature. Such are the intellectual pretensions and anti-sensual biases of our age.

"Why don't you write something that has less of a sexual emphasis?" I once asked him. "You use sex as a vehicle to talk about larger issues anyway. Can't you find a different context in which to discuss these things?"

"I'd like to," he answered, ever the pragmatist, "but this is sure money."

Rumor had it, recently, that he was no longer interested in writing what is commonly referred to as pornographic literature. "Good," I thought. "Something will replace it that will be reviewed more widely and that will gain Marco the success he so richly deserves." So when he phoned and asked me to write the introduction to his new book, I felt both honored and curious to see what he had come up with.

"What's it about?" I asked.

"Beyond bisexuality," he answered, "which also happens to be a tentative title."

"Oh," I said, my hopes for his career fading. "Then what do you need my introduction for? You're a far better writer on that topic than I am."

"But you're a medical doctor and a psychiatrist," he candidly countered. "A preface by you might lend the book a certain legitimacy and help sales. Besides which, you can write whatever you want to. Make it personal, clinical, whatever."

Flattered, I did not bother to inform him that my name on six previous books had not resulted in any best sellers. Instead, I accepted his offer, picked up the manuscript several days later, brought it home, and started reading. I soon realized that my solicitous concern for his career was unnecessary, for while this may be his last sex book, it is so different in scope and concept from his previous gothic novels that it simply has to be appreciated by a wider audience than is constituted by the usual stroke-book devotees.

I could, wearing my psychiatrist's hat, make a valid case for both the therapeutic and redeeming social value of a book that explores the areas beyond bisexuality. In that event I would confine my remarks to the collection of essays that comprise the second half of this work. I'd attempt to convince you that Doctor Vassi had advanced the work of Drs. Sigmund Freud and Wilhelm Reich to its logical conclusion. If the Great Repression we, as a society, suffer from is sexual, and if individual neurosis consists of the failure of libidinous energy to find its natural outlets, what more logical treatment is there than one which insists upon plunging into the phobicly avoided arena of eroticism? The fact that psychoanalysts have not urged such a straightforward and common sense approach bespeaks their own lack of daring and their own fear of social and professional ostracism. This timidity ought not to surprise anyone, for therapists are as mortal as the rest of us and very much the products and the tools of the conventional society that they serve. It takes an unusual person—be he sage or madman—to open our eyes to what is right before them. And Marco Vassi, though he has occasionally been thought so, is certainly no madman.

One must admire those who teach by example, not merely words, for the work that they do on themselves serves as an inspirational beacon to the rest of us. Marco's erotic adventures can only be seen, again and again, as attempts to transcend the limitations on freedom that Culture has imposed upon one and all. The discovery that yesterday's taboos are invalid is also the wedge in the door of authoritarianism, for it leads one to question similar Social divens in the realms of politics, science and progress.

I'd prefer, however, to go past my psychiatric evaluations in discussing ideas beyond bisexuality. For that, I must don my multicap of writer and reader. Why? Because psychiatry deals with one worrisome yet limited aspect of existence known as Mental Health, while Vassi's book encompasses existence itself.

"The sexual act," he wrote, "in all its forms has many layers of motivation." And it is his microscopic attention to and analysis of sexual detail that gives this work its extraordinary range.

Marco is not chronicling pathology nor is he writing merely about sex. Instead, lust and perversity serve as starting points which magnify larger existential issues such as love, roles, ego, meaning, and death. And it is all done with an unusual admixture of gentle cynicism, universal truth, and great good humor. When his business tycoon (*The Sicilians Revenge*) makes speeches on political power while receiving a blow job, a looking glass is held up revealing the idiocy of our manners and desires. Nor are these actions and motivations diseased in any way, reflecting, instead, the all too human absurdity in each of us.

And what a cast of memorable characters he creates in his fables, characters who mock all those conventional trappings and images we hold so dear. Do you want the inside scoop on Law and Order? Then read about the perverse policewoman in *Subway Dick*. Medicine? Get to know the *Dying Gynecologist* who enters his field not to save lives but to savor pussy. Higher Consciousness? Meet God, an unpretentious Jolly Green Giant who is as unaware of the facts of creation as the autistic onanist who he visits on earth in order to fuck.

Nothing is sacrosanct. We are perpetually provoked to examine and acknowledge the base within the sublime. Love gets its due in *Yesterday's Iago*. Sexuality itself is continuously poked fun at and nowhere as neatly as through the person of Butch Medusa—the sexual counterpart of Ian Fleming's

Dr. No—who produces the ultimate power machine: a Sexual Cyclotron. Innocents and revolutionaries a like have their come-uppance in *The Land of the Sperm King*. The Mental Health profession is dealt with through a renowned therapist who "traced all neurosis to the suppression of embarrassment people feel when farting," and consequently comes up with "the most revolutionary treatment in the history of psychology: Enema Therapy."

I laughed myself silly at several points throughout these tales, for Marco has a way of making us aware of our stupidities by placing existing conventions in surreal contexts. Who will forget the *Organic Coprophiliac*, a pseudo-Gothic tale set in middle America and told in the best Mary Shelley/Vincent Price manner, wherein Mother informs Daughter of a curse visited upon all the females in the family line? The great questions which follow concern very real customs, such as: When should you let a man shit in your mouth? After the first date or after you're engaged? And will he lose respect for you if you do it too early? Similarly, the bankruptcy of our policy of industrial progress is personified by an Italian Mafioso, whose phallus was "hard and gnarled like a De Nobili cigar."

Revolution through iconoclasm. That's what Marco Vassi is about. And gallows humor as he explores our ever-present human foibles.

One sees in Vassi Genet's Holy Degenerate, as he lovingly describes the grotesque. Or a sexual O'Henry in the twists and turns of his plots where lesbians are transformed into heterosexuals, killers into victims, and constables into perverts. Vidalesque playfulness emerges in *No Woman of Man Born*. And everywhere there is the mocking deliciousness of Rabelaisian grossness—peeing, farting, lapping, and shitting—which serves to underscore how our world of constructed manners still rests upon some basic animal functions. And all of this is brought together through a fine appreciation of the law of opposites; of the necessary juxtaposition of Yin and Yang.

Beyond bisexuality? Yes indeed. For Marco is not content with closing the distance between our male and female natures. It's something far broader than that he's after. He's out to heal the split between our sense of daring and our basic entropy, between our poetic visions and our gross bodily functions, between our existential awareness and our all too human limitations.

Marco Vassi, I thank you for letting me read and dedicate your book.

A CARCASS OF DREAMS

erotic fables for radical minds

*There is no better way to know death
than to link it with some licentious image.*
                              de Sade

The Dying Gynecologist

The dream of life was ending, and he was returning to the unformed state where consciousness could not follow. Having accepted the inevitability of this moment many years earlier, having made it a daily meditation, he was now without apprehension. If anything, he experienced a mild curiosity, faintly eager to experience the phenomenon of death.

For several hours he had lain in what appeared to be, to those gathered around his bed, a deep coma. But he was in fact fully awake. Having spent his entire career in the service of others, he gave himself permission to take these last few moments for himself, sinking lazily into his thoughts, savouring the voluptuous cadence of his breath, wandering down the corridors of memory to gaze upon the thing he had been, the infant, the boy, the man, and finally, the unencumbered organism coming to its predestined conclusion.

In the room sat his wife, his four children, his oldest friend. His favorite cactus plants had been moved in from his office so he might have the solace of their presence, reminiscent of the silences of the desert, the same silence he now prepared to enter. The six people waited, not speaking, wrapped in the wide calm that emanated from the man in front of them.

He felt no pain. The garment of flesh that had served him faithfully for so long had worn out and was ready to be discarded, to go back into the earth.

"I wonder what happens to the *I* in *me*," he said to himself, "to the intelligence that is even now asking the question. Is there any chance it might continue after the body ceases to function?"

As though in response, some strange sensation seized him, held him for an instant, and then disappeared.

"I'll know soon," he thought. "Or perhaps I won't know anything at all."

The situation amused him, and he smiled. The sudden appearance of the seemingly incongruous expression startled the others, who were watching him closely, half ashamed of their subliminal desire to have the whole thing over with. His eldest daughter leaned over and whispered in her mother's ear, "He must be a saint, to be able to smile on his deathbed."

"Wouldn't it be peculiar to die and find myself face to face with old Jehovah," the man thought. "Imagine all that nonsense turning out to be literally true. It's a mysterious universe, and anything is possible."

He chuckled, causing the hair to rise on the necks of the people around him.

The breath caught in his throat and his frame shuddered. There was no specific point at which he could grasp the unfamiliar process of passing away, but he knew that the moment of departure was very near.

"This is really very odd," he mused. "I can feel it happening, but it seems so distant, as though it had nothing to do with me at all. I don't feel like *I* am dying. There is just death going on, and I am one of the people observing it. The only difference between me and the others is that when it happens, they will stand up and walk out and I will be left lying here."

Then abruptly, as though he had fallen from a great height, he felt everything drop away from him. Time underwent a cataclysmic change, and he was swept by a sensation of rocketing through space at an exponentially increasing speed, until he was going faster than light itself. And yet, the faster he moved, the more still everything became. Opposites lost their identity.

One by one, his faculties shut down. Hearing, touch, taste, smell, all disappeared. His thoughts blew off his mind like shingles from a roof in a high wind. He opened his eyes for the last time.

"Sam," his wife said.

"Goodbye Constance," he croaked and saw nothing more.

Relinquishing everything he had ever imagined he might lay claim to in the universe, he bade farewell to himself. In a microsecond of utter clarity, he saw what an ironic play life was, what a strange dance of fantastic reality. Beyond all ability to apprehend his experience, he gave himself up to death.

But it was not yet time.

He lost awareness of the external world, and his breathing stopped, but the vital force which had animated the inert elements of his body and sustained the cohesion called existence had not yet dispersed. A doctor would have pronounced him dead, for his heart had stopped beating. But beneath the measureable manifestations, in the core of his being, the finest thread of electricity still hummed. All that he had been was now reduced to that single throb of energy.

Subjectively, it was like falling asleep, and into a dream. First, a total loss of self-consciousness, then a sentient blackness, and finally a slow discernment of form. A blank screen lit up, and on it appeared the thin line of a far distant horizon, such as the edge of ocean seen from shore. It separated sea from sky, both the same shade of deep cobalt blue.

For an eternity, nothing moved. And then, faintly, a dot emerged from ground into figure, balanced delicately on the line. Subtly, slowly, it grew larger, obviously coming closer to the shore where the man stood. Without any landmarks, there was no way to estimate its size. As the relatives and friend began to look at one another, attempting to decide who should approach the body to find out whether the end had come, the man began to hear the first low ripple of trumpets which seemed to accompany the object.

Now, measuring the thing against his own height, he was able to assess its scale. As the music swelled, a jagged burst of golden light shattered the scene, and he gazed up at what thunderously swept toward him, a thing a thousand feet high and perhaps a third as wide, taking up his entire field of vision. It flew forward with majestic ease until it stopped suddenly, a few feet in front of him, and his knees buckled when he realized what it was.

He looked up into the face of a giant, encompassing, and perfectly formed cunt, quivering in purple radiance, a great mandala enveloping him in its aura. He gazed upon it reverently. In smell, in texture, in pulsating vividness, it was the quintessence of cunt, ideal in its every fold, its every hue.

"My Lady," he whispered, and fell prostrate before it.

In the mind of the man within his mind, kneeling before his object of worship, he was twenty-five again, in his last year of medical school, wondering whether he should become a specialist or go into general practice. He was talking it over with a friend, when the young man told him, "Why don't you become a gynecologist. You're always complaining about how horny you are. If you become a cunt specialist, you won't have any trouble at all getting laid. Just think of all those women coming in and spreading their legs for you. And paying for it to boot!"

As the entire course of a great river can be traced to a tiny bend at its source, so his career was shaped by the offhanded bit of half-meant advice. He shaped his studies in that direction, giving his parents rationalizations which involved the greater profitability of that particular line of medicine, and within two years, he began practice.

His first patient had found him almost unbearably nervous. The woman was infected with some baroque venereal strain, and when she split herself apart on his table, the smell which seeped from the tainted organ caused him to retch. He was fortunate that she was a prostitute with no false modesty, and so was saved from embarrassment by her remarking, "Yeah, that's the way my clients feel. Can you fix it up, doc?"

He performed a series of tests, sent smears to the laboratory, and finally doused her with antibiotics, vaginal jellies, and suggestions for douching. A week later he saw her again and her cunt was as good as new. When he examined her the second time and pronounced her well on the way to cure, the gratitude in her eyes was as much payment as the money she gave him.

How many cunts had there been after that? Middle-aged housewives with bored cunts, young girls with puppydog cunts, whores with leathery cunts, nuns with pimply cunts, secretaries with pornographic cunts, witches with velveteen cunts, grandmothers with withered cunts, children with unarticulated cunts, passionate women with engulfing cunts. Cunts of a thousand eyes, cunts of a million moods. Smiling, pouting, shouting, brooding, yearning, burning, angry, gay, hungry, sad. Again and again the same single action—the legs swinging wide at his request, like the gates opening to the thief upon saying the magic words, "Open Sesame." He would first see the hair, sometimes sparse, sometimes thick, or coarse, or fine, or black, or golden, or red, or curled, or straight. And then the thing itself.

Where few men looked and few men touched, he prodded and pulled and stroked. He dove in with instruments, he slithered in with fingers. Sometimes he found disease, often he found nothing more than the desire to be entered. And when his hand came out it was not infrequently covered with secretions that were something other than the lubricating cream he had used to ease his penetration.

At the beginning he had kept what they had taught him in school was the proper professional distance. All the doctors had been trained to treat the cunt as something septic, something to be approached only with gloves on, with formal face and averted glance. Something to be pried apart with metal shoe horns. But he could not maintain that artificial pose for long. He loved cunts. That was the reason he had become a gynecologist: to see cunts, to touch cunts, to smell cunts, to heal cunts.

It was in the third month of practice that his first thrilling contact took place. The patient was the wife of a prominent psychoanalyst, in her early thirties. She came for a general checkup, saying she did it once a year and that his name had been recommended by a friend. She wore a tight sheath dress, outlining her ample buttocks, showing her bulging thighs, accenting her full breasts. She was a beautiful and sultry woman, and the doctor felt his cock stir at the thought that he would soon have her lying on her back, her legs hoisted over stirrups, and with what he knew would be a luscious cunt lying agape, waiting for him to minister to it. His lips trembled slightly as he spoke, so calmly, in such a sophisticated manner, saying all the lines proper to the doctor-patient scenario.

"It's amazing what you can get away with," he thought, "once you put it in a socially acceptable context."

In the examination room it went as he expected, except that

when it came time for him to slip on his plastic gloves, he boldly discarded the gesture. When he touched the fragile edges of her pink cunt, it was with his bare fingers. He seemed to enter some sort of trance, his ratiocinative faculties mesmerized. He entered a world of brute sensation, and without his understanding the process as such, his hands began a complex communication with her cunt. He found he was talking to her as he moved inside her, in a way that augmented the medical patter, the stock phrases . . . "does that hurt? is it sore there? this seems fine." When he stroked her cervix, it was not sex, and yet it was not not-sex. It was like the perfect edge of good massage, in which the mode is tactile ambiguity, where meaning and message continually interpenetrate.

A sigh escaped her lips. "She's enjoying this as much as I am," he thought, "and for the same reasons." Her cunt was already wet and the aroma it gave off was unmistakably erotic. His eyes moved from her cunt up past her belly between her breasts and into hers. She was watching him.

"Yes," she said.

He took off his clothes and fucked her as she lay. He came standing up.

From then on he fucked on the average of two women a day. Once he had broken through the convention of professional coldness, he was able to see with mounting acuity that at least half the women who came to him came simply to be caressed.

"Where are the men?" he said to himself over and over again. "Why isn't anyone loving these poor women?"

At first he made some mistakes, occasionally pushing for a sexual encounter when one hadn't spontaneously arisen, and he succeeded only in frightening the women involved. He often had doubts as to what sort of danger he might be in; might not a complaint end his career, or even land him in jail? Finally, he made peace with the fact that if he paid attention to business first, the business being the diagnosis and cure of disease, then whatever plums fell his way were his right to eat, and no bad fortune would be attached to that.

The woman he married was frigid. He chose her precisely because she was frigid. Examining her one afternoon, he saw that she had absolutely no sensation in her vagina. Her pelvis was locked in a chronic muscular spasm and her entire attitude was one of distaste for anything carnal.

"She's perfect," he thought, "she'll never bother me with excessive demands."

He courted her and married her and within a week after the ceremony she was overjoyed when he suggested separate bedrooms. He only fucked her about a hundred times in over thirty-five years, in groups of about twenty-five each, to conceive children. She settled into the role of mother and housewife, and purred in constant contentment that her husband allowed her to remain chaste.

Meanwhile, back at the office, he fucked himself silly.

By the time he was sixty, he had fucked more than fifteen thousand different women and had had his hands in the cunts of at least five times that many. "This is the best job a man could ever have," he told himself often, as his door opened, and his nurse ushered in yet another woman, and he would look at her the way a man looks at a woman's body in the street, calculating its curves, imagining its charms. But with a crucial difference.

"In a few minutes," he would think, "you're going to spread your legs for me, and offer me your cunt. And it will all seem very proper until I touch you a certain way, and you will realize that, all social rationalizations aside, you are opening your cunt to the eyes and fingers of a total stranger, a man you have never seen before, and one who, you will comprehend with a delicious shudder, wants to fuck you. And will we fuck? Or will I eat you out? Or will you suck my cock? Or will I have you get on your hands and knees so I can 'examine' you from behind?"

As the darkness of his death deepened, the memories faded, and the immense cunt before his mind's eye began to tremble, and open. From its roseate serrated center another cunt emerged, and another from the center of that. Cunt after cunt opened from the cunt preceding it. It was an infinite progression, never fully reaching him, continually spilling forth. He strained forward, to be taken into the heart of the budding cunt machine. It was the baby attempting to return, it was the man diving into the mystery, it was both and all.

And as he reached up in revery, the body on the bed bent at the middle and sat bolt upright. The people in the room were shocked at what they thought was a corpse perform such a sharp strenuous act. His lids flew up, but he saw nothing. His lips moved. A single word lept from his throat.

"Cunt," he said.

And from the depths of his desire, the face of death spun forward at lightning speed to snatch him in its jaws. What it looked like, no one will ever know, for death comes differently to each human being.

The gynecologist fell back on the bed. This time he was really dead. Those who heard his final word claimed that he had said nothing when people asked if he had said anything before he died. They did not understand what he meant, and ascribed it to delirium. It was given out to all his friends that he had died happy. As indeed he had.

In one of his notebooks there was found the notation, "There are too few doctors who remember the original reason for playing doctor."

Subway Dick

He may have seen her hundreds of times before he noticed her. Every weekday morning for over four years he had reached the Christopher Street station at a little after eight o'clock and stood with scores of others waiting for the train to take him to the world uptown where he spent half his waking hours, sitting in a cubicle, performing obscure and largely meaningless rituals with thousands of sheets of paper. Like the millions who descended daily into the tunnels to be shunted back and forth like cattle, he was usually in a foul mood. But the woman changed all that.

She had just lost a dime in a gum machine, and was standing in front of it, fuming and banging at the coin slot, when he passed by. Something about the quality of her energy at that point arrested him and he stopped to look at her. He drank in her features with a single visual gulp. But the subway car came thundering in and braked to a halt with a sickening screech of metal against metal, and he was jolted out of his stance. He did not think about her further that day.

The next morning, he saw her again, and once more swallowed her whole with his eyes. He stopped, taking a more detailed look at her, scanning her jet black hair, worn in a pony tail, her thin nose with flaring nostrils. Her body was wrapped in a thick winter coat, protection against the February cold. To his surprise, she glanced at him, her eyes oddly troubling, and then looked away.

During the next few weeks, although he made no special effort, he ran into her almost every morning. She was beginning to take on the air of an acquaintance. Once he started to greet her before he checked himself, remembering the strict New York etiquette which absolutely forbids talking to, smiling at, or in any way being friendly to other people on the street. It took him a while to realize that he was coming to relish seeing her, that it added a spark of interest to an otherwise dull and tedious beginning to his days.

By the end of March, he knew a good deal about her. The range of her wardrobe, the texture of her moods, the rhythm of her walk, had all been openly accessible to his study. It was amusing to speculate. Judging from the quality of her clothing, she probably made no more than a hundred and thirty dollars a week. She was probably a secretary. She wore no rings of any kind, and almost certainly lived alone. She used a minimum of makeup, a faint flush of lipstick and light eyeshadow. Her reading taste was random, as she might carry St. Augustine's *Confessions* one day and a popular book on astrology the next.

It wasn't until the first week in April that he felt a desire to get closer. The first day on which it was warm enough to do without a coat, she appeared in a tight skirt which outlined a full high ass and rounded thighs, and in a jacket which, when unbuttoned, showed breasts that were just large enough to fit into each of his cupped hands. The thinness of her mouth, at first glance giving her a prim look, now contrasted with the electric sensuality of her body. It occurred to him that it might be possible to fuck her.

That galvanized him into action.

From the status of a charming novelty to add a touch of mystery to his mornings, she became a goal, a prize for him to win. He began to get up earlier each day, in order to shower, to choose his clothes with care, and prepare his mood. He went through the mating ritual which is common to birds and fish and beasts that share the same biosexual heritage as humans. He thrilled to his own sense of purpose, and attempted to calculate whether she might find him attractive. Without describing it as such, he began to court her.

Hers was the stop before his. As the weather grew warmer and her clothing grew lighter, he arranged it so he stood closer to her in the tightly packed car. He was finally able to smell her perfume, mingled with the crisp aroma of her firm flesh. He was able to perceive the delicate whorls of her ears, the slight tensions in her throat as she swallowed. He wondered what her name was. He even became aware of her imperfections, and could judge from her complexion on which days she had her period. He also thought he could detect, from a general looseness and jauntiness in her manner, when she had fucked the night before. One Wednesday, he actually touched her, feeling the rough tweed of her skirt against the tops of his knuckles. His knees sagged and he had to grab the hanging support strap to keep from falling to one side.

That evening he pondered talking to her. It maddened him that, while on one level he knew her intimately, in terms of social intercourse they were total strangers. He had watched her walk across the platform and knew the way her buttocks jiggled as she moved, and yet he had not yet heard her voice. He considered that were he to speak to her, he might find her terribly ignorant. Too often in the past he had desired a woman's body and had his lust shrivel upon coming in contact with her mind.

"What if she is shallow?" he said to himself. And in the end decided not to make any overture just yet.

Wondering whether it was cowardice or wisdom that chose his course of inaction, he worked toward more physical contact without any formal introduction or exchange. The following morning he moved with the force and agility of a star halfback in arranging it so that he stood behind her without having drawn undue attention to himself. Sliding and jostling with consummate skill and experience, he followed her through the densely packed crowd until she stopped at one of the vertical support bars in the center of the car. He eased in close.

It had been subwaymanship of the first water, and no knight jousting for a lady's favor could have performed better. As the train pulled away from the station with its customary lurch and everyone in the car swayed with it, he looked down the length of his body. Her buttocks were less than an inch away from his cock.

"So near and yet so far," he thought. He dared not move.

The train gathered speed as it clanged toward fourteenth street. It hit a curve and once again the mass of humanity within its iron confines, like fluid in a container, rolled to one side. Unbelievably, and to his stinging joy, the twin mounds of her ass cheeks swung pendulously back and nestled for a brief tingling second in the hollow of his crotch. Fire alarm bells went off in his groin, and he was almost instantaneously erect, the bulging cock straining the fabric of his pants.

She did not touch him for the rest of the ride, and when he got to his office he went directly to the john where he sat, massaging his cock with quiet frenzy until the autonomous ejaculation relieved him of the almost unbearable pressure. The fleeting contact was enough to serve as fuel for the most outrageous fantasies. He imagined that her cunt was endowed with a special heat-generating faculty, that merely to be near it would be enough to trigger orgasm in an army of men. He went through the rest of his day in a stupor, relegating the tasks to be done to his instinctive center, and saving his intellectual ability to enrich the pictures in his mind.

The next day was a Saturday and he was too overwrought to spend the weekend alone. He knew he was at the edge of some mammoth foolishness, but he could not help himself. "I only rubbed against a woman on the subway," he repeated to himself, "I mustn't let it get blown all out of proportion." But the woman had been transmogrified into an *idee fixe*, and he was succumbing to its magnetic power. To ease his tension, he called an old girl friend and fucked her five times in the sixty hours he had to wait before he would see the lady of the subways again.

And when he did, he knew he was lost. She wore a skirt so tight, with material so thin, that both the outline and color of her panties could be seen. Her blouse was diaphanous, and he could make out the pale gold of her skin beneath it on both sides of the brassiere which cupped her breasts in its white plastic grip. Despite the debauch of the weekend, desire boiled in his blood.

The train moved smoothly, and he cursed the efficiency of the engineer. But just before thirty-third street, it stopped altogether, and the lights dimmed. There was a two-minute wait before the conductor's voice rasped over the loudspeaker, "There's a train stuck ahead of us, and we'll have a short delay." It was a crashing stroke of good luck.

His strategy was to try the *mano morte*, the dead-hand technique used by the Italians. The fingers are allowed to rest against the body of the target woman in such a way that there is no suggestion of attack. If she seems not to notice, the pressure can be gradually increased. If she fidgets, he can take refuge in the fact of the extreme crowding to silently plead innocence of wanting to have touched the delicious skin in front of him.

The middle knuckle of his middle finger came to rest exactly in the center between her buttocks, where the skirt pulled tautly over the valley. For a number of seconds he dared not even allow himself to feel the sensation, so delicate was his approach. Then, she shifted her weight, going from one leg to the other, and her cheeks moved, suddenly, grandly, sweeping across the width of his hand. A burbling moan of pleasure chugged to his lips, but he suppressed it sharply. He waited a short while, and then put his hand against her once more. Again she shifted, and again the treasured ass slid beneath his touch.

Now he was in a quandary. Was she unconscious of what was happening and moving randomly, or aware of his touch and showing her annoyance, or aware of his touch and cooperating in the encounter? It seemed as though his entire manhood was on the line. He had waited a very long time, and now was the moment to test their relationship. Boldly, he pulled back his hand and with a sense of historical finality, shuffled forward two tiny inches, just enough to ease the front of his body against her back.

Sheet lightning played over his sensorium. He was as alert and balanced as a man on a tightrope. She might whirl around and say something ugly, something terribly ugly, and inflict a wound on him that would take a long time to heal. Or she might respond to his overture. He waited, tortured by the suspense.

And upon that, quite easily, simply, and gently, she relaxed into her heels, throwing her weight back, and let her body rest with utter passivity against his. She had accepted the touch.

The train lept forward just as his erection began to poke into the space between her legs. They rode that way until reaching her stop, his cock sizzling with the secret contact in the packed subway car, while his face remained calm, his eyes darting about to see if anyone saw, and finding nothing but the stunned gazes of the city's wage slaves being transported to another day of empty drudgery. When they came to her station she stepped away from him quite deliberately and before getting off looked once over her shoulder and into his eyes. He could not tell what her expression meant.

It escalated rapidly after that. He was soon pressing into her very tightly, pushing his pelvis with tiny surreptitious strokes as she squeezed her buttocks and released them. On some days she wore no panties and he gave up his boxer shorts altogether. He almost screamed the day she reached behind her and caressed his cock with her hand.

They took to meeting at the back of the subway car so she could lean into the corner while he covered her. If he kept his raincoat on he could slip his cock out of his fly with no one seeing. One morning she wore slacks and he put his erection between her legs, coming in her woolly crotch as the train slugged its way uptown. They suffered a near fatal accident one morning when a young schoolboy, recklessly making his way from car to car, opened the connecting door and they almost pitched forward into the narrow platform. He had a wild impression of gleaming tracks before he recovered his balance and pulled himself back in, grabbing her waist to keep her from falling. The boy caught a glimpse of his cock and blinked in disbelief before a slow smile spread over his face and he whispered, "Sorry to crash in on your party, mister."

Still, he was loathe to speak to her. "What can I possibly say at this point?" he thought. "We've already progressed beyond conversation." And then, "Why spoil a good thing? If we start dating, instead of being the most extraordinary experience of my life, she'll show up as just another woman."

He was amazed that the affair had progressed from discovery to infatuation to consummation to cynicism so effortlessly, and all within the parameters of an eight-minute subway ride.

Yet, what could be accomplished in the crowded car was painfully limited, and he was bursting for a more total encounter. Then one morning, as he waited for the train, he saw her standing next to the women's toilet. She nodded, and he edged toward her. She backed up, put a nickel in the slot, and opened the door, beckoning him to follow. Like one in a trance he moved past her into the tile room. She slammed the door behind them and jammed the lock with a piece of metal.

They were alone in the white gleaming cubicle.

"This is insane," he hissed, the first words he had ever spoken to her.

By way of reply she peeled off her clothes. He watched mesmerized as the long-desired body appeared before him. When she was naked she abruptly threw herself at his feet, begging him to fuck her. She tugged at his pants and licked his shoes, rolling across the filthy floor. The woman of his dreams lay before him, a panting slut, fingering herself shamelessly.

Propelled from the mundane to the baroque with such rapidity that the pulse in his temples began pounding painfully, he tried to put the event in some context. But it was all exploding too quickly, too forcefully. The girl groaned with desperate want and he could do nothing but succumb to the moment.

The many months of slow building broke in the instant, and for the following five minutes they did practically everything possible for a man and a woman to do together, playing out Krafft-Ebbing and the Kama Sutra at high speed. At one point she lay bent over the porcelain pissoir, her face in the water, as he whipped her with his leather strap. Some instinct told him he would never have another chance with her and that he had to get it in all at once. And it was not until he found himself foolishly ejaculating in her right ear that he came to his senses, aghast at the situation he found himself in.

He stepped back and leaned against the wall; he was slightly delirious. The woman dressed. When she was ready, he fumbled for something to say before they left the john. But his eyes grew wide as she reached into her purse and pulled out a police badge and a .357 Magnum revolver.

"You're under arrest," she said. And added, "I've had my eye on you for some time now."

The case, when it finally appeared, was thrown out of court. The city, due to the uproar being raised by Gay Activists' Alliance, was enjoying a spell of liberalism in what were technically considered sex crimes. The judge ruled that the man was a victim of vice squad entrapment, and, as such, his arrest was unconstitutional.

He was so shaken by the entire course of events that he moved to San Francisco. He was just recovering from his ordeal when he learned they were planning to build a subway there. He then jumped off the Golden Gate Bridge.

The woman began another long lonely vigil, seeking sex offenders in the tunnels beneath the city, riding the rails until some man touched her, and then rubbed his cock against her, letting him have his way until he was fucking her and stomping her and pissing on her and doing god-awful things to each of her orifices, at which point she would arrest him. She felt that sex was holy, and had chosen her job to keep it that way.

Land of the Sperm King

In a valley not far from where the mythical realm of Shangri La was reputed to have been, there flourished a people who lived for almost three thousand years without a government. They had no laws, no organization of any kind, and were guided by a spiritual leader who was chosen from among the children born on the day of the winter solstice, each serving for life, and then passing the mantle on to whichever of the eligible candidates gave the wisest answer to the secret question, which only kings and queens could ask. The leader, when he or she was close to death, would have all those born on the shortest day over the years of his or her reign gather in the wood outside the village, see them one by one, and decide who was to succeed to the position of eminence.

It was a strange role, for in no one's memory did the guide ever have to do anything. There were never more than several thousand people in the land; children were considered such rare and wondrous creatures that there was a trembling hesitancy about bringing them into the world. Everyone ate the same thing: fruits and nuts which fell from the trees, and a form of yoghurt made from goat's milk. They all drank the highly mineralized water that flowed from the mountains. They never killed anything. Their clothes were made from the skins of animals that had died a natural death. They did not work, except to fashion garments and cups, and build shelters to live in. They had no formal sports, although wrestling was popular, as was reindeer riding, climbing, and swimming.

Among them were a few who grew up with a deep inner distance from the others, and they spent most of their time alone, fashioning drums and flutes from wood and hides, giving the others music. Some made strange shapes out of clay and gave the others images to ponder. Some appeared periodically to tell long stories in hypnotically rhythmic language, speaking of things no one had ever experienced but which sounded mysteriously familiar.

When the spirit moved the guide, he or she would begin to dance, and then a feast would take place, the people making a fire and brewing tea from a grass that grew on the far side of the mountain that overshadowed their land, a drink with magic powers of intoxication. Sometimes the celebration would last for days, until the entire population had been so perfectly unified in a vortex of energy by the sacred dance and the sheer power of their massive gathering, that the field they moved in became the scene of a single orgiastic organism, pulsing in ponderous and quickening tempo.

Generally, however, they spent their time contemplating the wonder of creation.

The guide possessed one idiosyncrasy as a mark of office; he or she ate nothing but sperm. In fact, to the degree that the people had a formal culture at all, it centered around providing the guide with enough to eat. Since sperm is a perfect food, the guide needed nothing else. And since the people lived a rarified existence, eating only the purest foods, drinking only the most vital water, breathing only the sharpest air, and since they were exposed to nothing but peaceful manifestations of the life energy, they were as sensitive as flowers in their capacity to take nourishment directly from the sun. It is not surprising that the guide's daily intake was relatively small, usually amounting to no more than the combined volume of seventeen ejaculations.

Over the span of history, of course, different guides developed individual feeding habits. The conventional method was for male guides to use the cunts of young maidens as cups, having the day's male volunteers mount the female volunteers and make love lustily until orgasm, at which point the guide would put his mouth to a succession of still hot trembling vaginas and suck the sticky deposit from the freshly fucked lips. Most of the female guides took their sperm straight, lying languidly on a couch while the day's complement masturbated over her and at the moment of climax putting the spurting cocks into her waiting mouth. There were what the people called "interesting" guides, men who sucked the sperm directly from cocks, and women who preferred using cunts as a vehicle.

Occasionally there would be a guide who developed more esoteric tastes and might request a daily dollop of yak sperm. One guide took a fancy to tiger sperm, and since the people were so gentle they could approach the fiercest beasts and coax the vital fluid from them, the wish was able to be granted. That particular guide was legendary for his sexual prowess, for after half a cup of tiger sperm he was able to fuck twenty women to satiation without stopping once. Another guide, a woman, ate only hummingbird sperm, and before she died had become totally transparent.

It never occurred to anyone at any time that things should be different. They were the only people in the history of the species who did not let the acquisition of language rob them of their primal simplicity, and so they attained true human dignity. Possessing wisdom, they had little use for knowledge; living in a state of tranquil bliss, they had no inclination to intensity of purpose. They watched the universe in its constant infinite turnings and workings, understanding that they were blessed just to be alive and know the wonder of it all. In touch with the primordial realities of the cosmos, they were beyond the superficialities of civilization.

It is conjectured that they were the descendants of a small band of people that followed Lao Tzu out of China after he wrote his *Tao Te Ching*. Instead of going to the mountains to die, as legend has it, he went to live. Leaving China at the age of eighty-five, he continued for another sixty-three years, teaching the people non-ado. So powerful was his influence that it sustained them for almost three millennia.

In the seventeenth century of the Christian era as measured by western calendars, they were visited by two Dominican priests who came upon their valley by accident. The men were scandalized by what they considered obscene rites and general godlessness. They attempted to preach the gospel, but were met by a respectful indifference. They became an odd sight, flapping furiously about in their black and white robes, brandishing crucifixes, waving their bibles in the air, shouting at the people to put their clothes on and repent. It must be admitted that it was difficult to preach hellfire and brimstone to a people who had no concept of sin except "doing what is unnecessary," a faculty the priests excelled in. But the people were willing to let them be, viewing them as merely one of the more bizarre manifestations of the unfathomable universe.

The missionaries were able, however, to test the tolerance of even this ultimately benign people, first by chopping down living trees to make a dead church, and then by running through the grove where the guide was awaiting his daily meal and lashing the backs of the happy fuckers who were preparing his food. The people, for the first time in centuries, were confused, and they asked the guide what they should do, an action no guide in anyone's recollection had been asked to perform.

He thought about it a while and requested that the priests be restrained. Then, hoping to pierce to the core of the situation, he asked two of the young maidens to draw forth some sperm from their bodies so he might take their measure. The priests howled with outrage at the tender ministrations being given them by the gentle fingers and loving tongues of the women. And when they came, it was with horrible curses mingled with terrible prayers.

The king tasted each of their deposits and retched violently.

"These men are . . . " he began to say, and then paused, not having a word for the concept "depraved." He spit out the sperm and pondered for a while. "Take them to where the eagles nest," he said at last, "and push them from the mountain."

The priests were disposed of and the people remained undisturbed for another four hundred years.

Yet, their time was marked. In one of the wars which continually erupted about them, their valley was discovered by a platoon of Chinese soldiers. Shortly thereafter, they were descended upon by a delegation from the People's Republic, and told that they were to be liberated from the chains of spiritual autocracy and introduced to the wonders of democracy.

"You will be removed from your primitive state," the directive read, "and given factories and schools and police. Women will be free and allowed to work side by side with men. Everyone will learn to read and illiteracy will be eliminated." Finally, they were informed, they would elect their own representative to sit in the People's Assembly in Peking. Beyond that, they would be taught how to farm, pen animals, make iron, and build roads.

The people were stunned. The night the representatives left, with word that they would return in a week with soldiers, planners, teachers, officials, and anthropologists, the guide summoned the entire village.

"There is no way to know why these things happen," he said. "It is like watching the night sky and seeing a star suddenly plunge into the darkness of space. It is our time to be destroyed, and there is nothing we can do."

He stroked his wispy beard. "For myself, I will not live to serve those smiling and well-intentioned brutes who think their primitive machinery is superior to our formless understanding. I will go to the place of the eagles and throw myself into the air which is the sustainer of us all. You may come with me, or you may stay here, and learn to survive amidst the stupidity which is fast descending upon us."

He sat silent for a long while and then his face brightened. "Yet, we still have seven sunrises and seven sunsets. Time enough for eternity." And with that he jumped to his feet and began to dance.

The morning of the day when the delegation was scheduled to arrive, the entire people, spent from the continuous orgy of the previous week, went to the nearby mountain top. They sat in a loose circle and entered a state of communion, sharing their vibrations, sharing their breathing, their awareness. Finally, the guide stood up and walked to the edge of the precipice. As he stared down, a small boy's voice called out to him.

"Before we all return to the flow, can you tell us what the secret question is?"

The guide turned around and looked into the child's open face. "There is only one question," he said slowly, "and that is this.

"Why are there no questions at all?"

The boy's lips began to move and he started to speak. But then as though a light had gone on within the light of the sun, his entire expression changed and became one of perfect understanding. His face relaxed and his eyes grew soft. He looked back at the guide, and said nothing.

The guide smiled.

"Yes," he said to the boy and to the whole people, "the answer is not to say the answer, but to be the answer." And then to the child alone, "You might have been guide after me."

And with a cry of rapture, he threw himself off the cliff.

One by one and two by three they followed, until the last man and woman stood looking down at the rocks below.

"When we die, there will be no humans left," she said.

"Then so be it," he told her. "It is as the guide has said: it is our time to be destroyed."

They too flew into the void, and when the Chinese arrived that afternoon they could not make sense of what had happened. They made an official report to their headquarters, and by the time the sun had set they had planted their flag and given the place a name, something that no one had ever bothered to do before.

No Woman of Man Born

She stared into the mirror for a quarter of an hour, taking inventory, integrating the perceptions.

The legs are long and muscular, the shoulders broad, the hips narrow. The skin on her face is delicately etched, the result of two years of electrolysis. Straight black hair to the base of her neck, covering her ears, curling around her throat. Breasts curved like soft sherbet, the children of injected hormones. She is a handsome woman, as once she was a pretty man. Her ass is androgynous, and between her thighs, the infolded scrotal sac.

"I have done it," she thought. "At last I have a body to match my desires."

She ran her hands over her belly and cupped her breasts, stroking the nipples with her fingertips. They wrinkled, and stretched taut. She smiled.

"Alexandra," she said out loud. "Men will want you." And with that did a slow bump and grind for her reflection in the glass, all the while hugging herself with satisfaction.

As with all transsexuals, her road had been painful and difficult. For her entire youth and young manhood, she was unable to understand herself as anything but a homosexual, a condition she despised. Impotent with women, she had been, as a man, wretched in her need for men. And after many years of therapy, she came to accept that the condition of homosexuality was intractable.

The conclusion that followed, while logically ineluctable, had been for a long time too frightening to consider seriously. The existential force of having one's penis cut off shook her to the roots of her being. But her torment knew no surcease, and the choice between radical change and suicide became quite clear. She opted for the former.

She began tentatively, making enquiries, writing letters of application to doctors who had performed the process of transformation. Before long, the fantasy began to precipitate a reality, and she found herself having interviews with psychologists, talking to other transsexuals who had come out the other side, several in each of the two directions, and finally entered the actual mechanics of transition, beginning with hormone shots, hair-removal, special counseling, and on one unforgettable day, the first operation. And with all this, lessons on how to dress, how to move, how to speak, how, in short, to behave like a woman.

It had taken three years to reach this point, watching the final result in a mirror. A miracle had been performed, and it seemed to throw open a sparkling new world. She could enjoy men at last, as she always had, but now freely and openly, without the homosexual guilt she had never been able to shake off. She understood that from a certain viewpoint, her present condition might be considered even more pathological than the former one. But she didn't *feel* ashamed, and it is one's feeling about oneself that, in the last analysis, is the basic criterion for all judgement.

Now, when she flirted with a man, it would be as a woman. And when she gave head, it would be a woman's lips around the cock she sucked. Her face would be smooth, powdered, her mouth slightly rouged. Her chest would hold a woman's breasts for a man to fondle, and while the nipples would never yield milk, that would make no difference to her or to the man who was taking his pleasure with her. And when a man fucked her, it would be as a woman that she received him, and not as a "pervert," the word she had always used to describe herself. And after all this, she had, instead of the embarrassing penis, a cunt opening into her body, not as pretty as a real cunt, nor with a real cunt's smells and juices, but for all that, something that would serve. Its very artificiality, in fact, might give it a power of attraction and appeal that no real cunt could have.

"After all," she reasoned, "there can't be more than a couple of hundred artificial cunts in the whole world." She consoled herself that rarity overshadowed any intimations of the grotesque.

She opened the closet door on which the mirror hung, and began to choose her attire for the day. While recuperating from the final operation, she had not gone out or seen anyone, wanting to make her entrance into society all at once, whole and resplendent. She dressed beyond her usual simple taste, knowing that she was overdoing it, but unable to resist the temptation to go out in full drag.

"But it's not drag any more," she exclaimed. She was no longer a man, and the nylon stockings and panties and garter belt and brassiere and slip and dress and earrings and nail polish and lipstick and pumps and eyeshadow were now her legitimate clothing. A rush of excitement surged through her as she thought of bathing suits and the beach, of tight slacks and swinging her hips as she walked.

And for an instant, she even thought of Ralph, her friend for so many years, the man she loved more than anyone in the world, but to whom she could never venture a physical overture. Ralph had known that she was homosexual, and it had not affected their friendship, which was based on an intellectual affinity. Still, he had made it clear that he could not consider her sexually. During the time she was undergoing her transformation she had asked him, "Do you think you might desire me when I am a woman?" And he had not replied for a long time, then answered, "It might be possible. I don't know. It's extraordinary just to think about, but I won't know until I see you in your new body."

Now, glorious in full regalia, she looked at herself once more, and a well-dressed, very attractive woman of about thirty-five looked back, and winked. She was feeling just the tiniest bit randy already.

"Would you like to go for a drink?" Alexandra said to her image.

"And perhaps meet a man?" the image asked.

"Or should I call Ralph?" Alexandra replied.

"Not yet," her image told her, "you need some experience first."

Alexandra felt a shiver go down her spine as the impact of

the reality she had become grazed her deepest sense of self. She checked herself out one last time, picked up her handbag, and walked out the door to see what the world had to offer.

As she stepped into the street, apprehension gripped her. At the back of her mind was the thought that someone would notice, would point to her and say, "Look, there's a transsexual." She glanced down to see if her slip was showing, and the already conditioned gesture of a woman brought her new courage.

She attracted no attention at all, except the routine stares of men who looked at her breasts as she approached and at her ass as she went by. She had to suppress her exuberance which threatened to propel her into long striding steps, and remember to walk as her coach had taught her, keeping her awareness on the sensation of her thighs rubbing against one another.

"Stay with your feeling of sensuality," he had told her, "that will keep you from reverting to masculine mannerisms."

Feeling more and more secure, strolling down the sidewalk as though she were a queen dressed as a commoner, her royalty apparent to no one but herself, she turned into one of those small dark restaurants which dot midtown. She stood uncertainly in the doorway for a moment, and was taken with a small edge of panic when the floor manager came up to her and said, "Will there be just yourself, madame?"

Madame!

She smiled graciously. "Just a drink, please, I won't be having lunch," she said, using the voice the same teacher had coached her in, making her sound a little like Marlene Dietrich with a bad cold.

He led her to a tiny round table, and she lit a cigarette to steady her nerves as the waiter brought her a Brandy Alexander, a drink she had always felt diffident about ordering when she went about in a man's body. She sipped slowly, relishing the fact that she left lipstick marks on the glass. Her joy was total, and she was torn between wanting to weep and wanting to throw up her arms and shout with pleasure.

Instead, she looked around discretely, and several tables away a man of about forty, dark and rugged, wearing a very expensive suit, was looking at her with an unmistakeable glint of desire. He was exactly her type, the kind of man who, when she had been a man, she would have done anything to have, and then have felt guilty about wanting. But now she could accept his overture, talk to him, and swim in his hunger for her. She would have to go slowly, waiting for the proper mood to tell him that she was a transsexual. And if he still wanted her, then she would have him, have a man at last, freely, openly.

She began to return his stare, but felt herself floundering in her response. She could not smile, nor lower her lids, nor shift her body, nor give any of the clues women use when they want to tell a man they're interested. She looked away in confusion.

"What's wrong?" she wondered. "Why don't I respond?"

She was about to ascribe it to nervousness in her new role when she realized that she was not really reciprocating his desire, and could find no feeling upon which to mount even a seductive glance. Intellectually, she could tell herself why she should desire him, could remember that there was a time when she would have been attracted to him, but now, he had no more sexual appeal to him as a woman than women used to have for him as a man.

She bent her head over her drink, pondering the strangeness of the situation, and was lost deep in thought when she sensed someone sitting across from her, at her table. Her heart skipped as she guessed it might be the man, and she didn't know how to deal with him.

But when she looked up, she found a woman looking back at her. A slim, well-groomed, utterly composed woman, who wore no makeup, and was dressed in a tightly cut suit. Her hair was short and her eyes were very very knowing.

The woman smiled, an expression that flushed through Alexandra like the embrace of a hot bath after a long stiff walk on a winter day. Her limbs grew weak, and the rest of the restaurant faded into distant obscurity, behind the irresistible magnetism of the woman who sat before her.

"I've been watching you," the woman said. "It was clear that you had no interest in that man who's been trying to catch your eye."

Alexandra knew at once that the woman was a lesbian, knew at once that she was making an overture, and knew at once, with stomach-shrinking certainty, that her new body was responding.

The homosexuality had pursued her through the entire change of gender, and in her transformed loins there flickered the familiar flame of an old, forbidden desire.

The Organic Coprophiliac

Wendy delicately shaded the corner of her mouth with her lipstick brush, took a long deep look at herself in the professional make-up mirror with the tiny frosted bulbs all around the edge, and smiled radiantly. From her sequined shoes to her beehive hairdo, she was perfectly rendered, ready to win all glances at the Senior Prom. The other men would neglect their dates just to have a dance with her, and she would flirt outrageously with them, knowing all the while that no matter who held her in his arms, only Jeff could hold her in his heart.

"Jeff," she whispered, and her fingers trembled at his name. Tall, rugged Jeff, with his lopsided grin and his playful blue eyes, his electrifying figure on the football field and his deep love of humanity which would one day earn him the initials M.D. after his name. She rubbed the pin he had given her just six months earlier, on that night when the moon had lit up the waters of the reservoir as they sat in his Maserati and he spoke those fateful words in her ear.

"Be mine," he had said. And hot scalding tears of joy had spilled from her eyes.

Now she stood up, regarding her young figure in the glass. The wide gown hid her long shapely legs, shaved and oiled for the night's special date. Her waist was narrow and flared quickly to pearl-white breasts that swelled over the tops of her bra cups. No man had ever seen her nipples, or put his hands on the sweet mound between her thighs. She was more than a virgin; she was a consciously constructed landscape of hesitant delights, nurtured and guarded, prepared for the appearance of the single gardener who would enter some day to gather up the fragile buds of her tender flowers. She had been kissed so few times that her lips still tingled when another mouth brushed hers. And no fingers had ever traced the luscious curve between her firm full buttocks.

"But tonight," she breathed, and trembled over the expanse of her entire body at the thought of what the night would bring.

There was a light tap at the door and her mother came timidly into the room. The two women looked into one another's eyes through the mirror, and then Wendy turned.

"Mother," she gushed, "I'm so happy."

"And I'm happy for you," her mother replied. "It seems just like yesterday that I was standing where you're standing now, thinking about the man who was to become your father."

"We've lived in this town a long time, haven't we?" Wendy asked in that solemn voice which always overtook her when she thought of her American heritage.

The older woman swept forward and held the young girl by the arm. Her face was troubled. She had the look of a person who was about to enter into a necessary but difficult conversation.

"There isn't much time before Jeff gets here to pick you up," she began, "and there's something I need to talk to you about."

"I think I know what it is," Wendy said, spinning out of her grasp.

"You're thinking of letting him do it tonight, aren't you? You're planning to go *all the way*!"

"Please, mother," Wendy pleaded, "I'm a grown woman. It's time I decided these things for myself. And I do love him. Don't spoil it by trying to argue me out of it."

"No, no, it's not that. I would be the last to try to dissuade you. After all, I did . . . the same thing, the night of my Senior Prom."

"You?" Wendy asked, aghast.

"I was young once too," her mother said. She eased Wendy into the rocking chair that had been in their family for a hundred and twenty-seven years. "I just want to be sure you're careful. And perhaps if I tell you a little story, it will help you understand." The woman sat down opposite her daughter, and began a tale which her mother had told her, and had been told by her mother before her, insuring that each generation was aware that its children did not lose the historical continuity which kept the blood line strong.

"It was your great grandmother who was first seized by the seemingly irrational desire to eat shit," the older woman said. "In those days, people didn't have the enlightened attitudes we have today, and what with killing Indians and chopping down trees, there just wasn't time for bedroom finesse. Lil was seventeen when she got married, as cheery a cherry as you are right now. Her husband was a good man, dependable, but boorish. She didn't even know how to broach the subject of her secret desire to him.

"One day, while he was off on a four-day hunting trip, a knife-grinder came by their house. She describes him in her diary as gaunt and salacious, and adds, 'just what I was looking for'. She invited him in for lunch, and when they were finished eating, she blurted out what she wanted from him."

Wendy paled. Like many young people, it was almost inconceivable to her that what she had looked upon as an intensely private urge might be commonplace to the rest of humanity. Her mother's voice went on, describing what their ancestor had done, but she heard little of the narrative, her own mind being filled with the image she had cherished for so long.

She saw herself lying on a couch, her skirt hiked up over her thighs, her cunt redolent with pungent slime, toes curled in anticipation. Above her, his piercing eyes boring into her tender flesh, Jeff bears down, his great buttocks crushing her cheeks, his terse anus pressing against her sweet innocent lips. And then, with a subtle shift, the passage begins. She gasps, she moans, she faints, and in succumbing, her mouth falls open. He pushes down, and with a fanfaronade of aggressive thoughts, voids his bowels on her immaculate face. She tries to escape, knowing all the while that she does not want to escape. She chokes as the hot suffocating mass slides onto her tongue, into her throat, and down her chest, scorching her lungs and filling her body with the vile and glorious fulfillment she had always understood would be hers. She cries out and rises to actively cover the pulsing hole, stretching her lips until they crack, sucking the final product of the body she loves until she almost bursts from lack of breath, as she combines the lowest servility with the highest daring, the profoundest love with the most scarifying sensuality.

She looked up out of her revery and into her mother's smiling face. The woman seemed to be reading the pictures in her mind. Wendy blushed.

"There's no way to explain it, really," she said. "Doctor Cory thinks that the desire is an inherited characteristic. It just seems to run in the family."

Wendy began to speak, hesitated, and then began again. "But I'm not the only one," she said. "Most of the other girls talk about the same thing."

"They're not allowing sex education in the classrooms, are they?" her mother shot out, ready to be incensed at the notion that the board of education was usurping what she believed to be the duty of parents.

"No," Wendy told her. "We get together at the soda shoppe and talk about our feelings. You know how girls do. And just yesterday Clarissa asked me whether I thought it was all right to let a boy shit in your mouth on the first date."

"In my day a girl would want at least an engagement ring before she'd let a boy take such liberties."

"I think so too, and that's what I told her. I think a girl and boy should know each other for a few months at least, and be going steady, before they get that intimate. But at least half the girls think that's old-fashioned."

"Well, times do change," her mother sighed philosophically. "But they'll learn the value of holding certain things back unless a man is extra good to them. If a woman gives a man everything at once, she has nothing to manage him with. You may not think that's important now, but wait until you've been married a few years."

"I don't know if I can hold myself back," Wendy pleaded.

Her mother took Wendy's hands between her own and held them to her breasts. "Jeff's a good boy," she said, "and I'm sure he's serious about your relationship. Just be careful, that's all."

"Will you give me some advice?" Wendy asked, capitulating at last to a recognition of superior wisdom in this area on the part of her mother.

"Well," the woman said, "make sure he doesn't eat spicy food or drink too much early in the evening. If he gets the runs it will ruin it for both of you. And don't get shit on your dress. It's almost impossible to wipe off and you'll stink all the way home. Make sure he doesn't think you're too easy or he'll lose respect for you."

Wendy put her head on her mother's shoulder. "I'm so lucky to have such an understanding mother," she said.

"My mother did the same for me," the older woman went on. "And you might as well start practicing how to cook from now on. After you're married you'll have to be very careful about his diet. See that he gets enough roughage. And feed him the healthiest food you can. You might as well be getting some good shit from him if you're going to get any shit at all."

Wendy's mother stepped back and the two women gazed at each other with moist eyes. "My little baby's going to be all grown up after tonight," the older woman said.

"You're the best mother a girl could ever want," Wendy told her.

Just then the door swung open and a man walked into the room. Portly, red-nosed, and kindly, he beamed at the picture before his eyes.

"Daddy!" Wendy squealed.

"That Jeff certainly is a lucky man," he said, looking at his daughter's shining face. And then he turned to his wife and in a gruff jocular tone asked, "Is there any chance of getting something to eat around here tonight?"

Wendy and her mother looked at one another for a few seconds, and then burst out laughing, leaving the man smiling in gentle confusion. He and his wife had had separate bedrooms for almost five years, and for him the ingestion, digestion, and elimination of food was no longer a process that held any trace of erotic passion.

Bluebeard's Instant Grecian Urn

Paul thought he knew why women resisted, and his unwillingness to let any external reality alter the system of his perception was, paradoxically, his greatest advantage over them. He lived in a world of images, and ruthlessly imposed his projections on everyone in his life in order to attain his ends. He had no feeling for women as autonomous creatures, but worshipped them passionately as objects of desire. He easily equated conquest with caring.

For him, a woman's sexual response functioned exactly like a neural synapse, in an all-or-nothing manner. In the same way that a large number of electrical stimuli build a charge that, at a crucial moment, fires the spark across the gap between nerve endings, a series of fucks would mount a readiness until, with shocking speed, the woman would surrender to her most uninhibited expressions. Generally, women held back, even in orgasm, sensing that once they let go, an unfathomable chasm would open up, and all that could save them from dissolution would be the continued attention from the man who brought them to that condition. They would then be, for all practical purposes, in his power.

Paul was an expert at enticing women to disregard their warning systems, their memories of broken hearts, betrayals, refusals; he was a master at pushing them to the edge of the erotic abyss and seducing them to leap. His was the knack of easing women into insouciance, yielding their essence to his demand. For Paul, only that moment of yielding counted. Before she surrendered to her need in his arms, a woman was an object of dalliance; and afterward, she had nothing further to reveal.

He possessed a rare combination of genius and lasciviousness. He might have modelled himself on de Sade, except that he lived in a technological era, and looked upon tying virgins to stone walls in hidden crypts with a certain condescension. He had more sophisticated machinery at his disposal.

From the first moment, when he was just nineteen, that a woman let drop the veils of her public countenance and revealed the terrible beauty of a face that had become no more than a pool within which to see the rigors of a soul in ecstasy, he knew that nothing else in life would have any real value for him. He dedicated himself to the elicitation of that brief moment when absolute openness flowered before his eyes. No priest ever served any god better than Paul the cultivation of women.

In the course of a decade he had found hundreds of them. He learned exactly how to manipulate himself to get them to offer their treasure to his insatiable eyes. He was handsomely endowed, a little over six feet tall, his body combining the best features of a lumberjack and a Martha Graham dancer. He wore his blond hair slightly long, and spent six hours each week at a gym, in narcissistic contemplation of his muscular development, as he lifted weights, swung on trapeze bars, or swam lustily in the pool. Otherwise, he was at work, doing a job which bored him, but which allowed him to live in fairly opulent fashion. After having taken a Ph.D. in molecular chemistry, he landed a position at Johnson and Johnson, joining a vast staff of laboratory workers whose projects included searching for ways to produce more long-lasting glue for Band-Aids.

At night, he fucked.

He continually looked forward to the bliss of having an attractive and intelligent woman squirming under him, his cock splitting her throbbing cunt, her fingers raking his shoulders, her legs shamelessly pulling him more deeply into her, and through it all her face a mask of capitulation to unholy joy. It was the face, more than the mere sensations of the act, which transported him. When the stilted mask of civilized appearance melted and the beast emerged, the angel could be born. And if she were, in her daily life, ultra sophisticated, ultra chic, then when she broke, he was blessed with seeing the contrast between that artificiality and the ultimate gift that can ever be given to man: the perception of the naked female soul.

But it was all so fleeting! He might watch a woman edge her way toward frenzy, see her hover at the very brink, and then go wild with the joy of wanton release. As the deep-chested howls burst from her throat, he could hold her only a few seconds, using his entire body as a feedback mechanism to orient the angle and intensity of his cock and thrust so that he extracted the maximum response, before she slipped into an orgasmic fury so private that the shades came down once more over her eyes. There were never more than those few brief moments during which he could gaze upon her, with the wrapt expression of a saint in the midst of a beatific vision. And then it was gone. Gone forever.

"If only there were some way to preserve the stickiness indefinitely," he heard a colleague say one afternoon during a seminar on the relationship between the respective surface tensions of skin and plastic.

"Preserve!" The word echoed in his mind.

"Yes," he thought, "if only I could preserve that instant."

That night he cancelled his date in order to ponder the implications of his insight. "What if I could," he mused, "freeze the woman at the very second she is producing the expression which is her most perfect, her highest manifestation of beauty?"

He thought of photography, but discarded the idea. A two-dimensional representation was not what he wanted. He desired the real thing. His mind lept from personal to social ramifications. "I would not only possess the thing that is most precious to me in the world, but will have created a work of supreme art, and in the process have immortalized a woman who would otherwise have passed into oblivion unknown. Such a piece would make the Mona Lisa seem the work of a primitive."

He was quite mad, of course, but also extremely brilliant, and with the resources of one of the nation's foremost chemical plants at his disposal, he was soon experimenting with a formula that would have the properties he required of it. It would have to be liquid, for he saw that he would need to use a syringe. It would have to work instantaneously, to keep the body he used it on in semblance of the full flush of life. And it would have to penetrate to every last cell of the person's physical structure.

Fired by the flames of monomania, he poured his genius into the project, and within a year he was ready to make his first try.

He decided to start with Cathy. He had been fucking her desultorily for several months, and she had peaked rather early in the affair. It was only a sentimental fondness for her that kept him seeing her. She was still capable of producing first-rate expressions, especially in the way her lips fell open after he came in her mouth, allowing his sperm to dribble down her cheeks and over her chin. He had seen that half a dozen times already. Her orgasm expression was neo-classic, the suggestion of pain in her furrowed brow contrasting exquisitely with the sucking gesture of her lips. After considering all contingencies, he decided to attempt to capture her reaction to being fucked in the ass. Primarily because the hypodermic would be easier to use if he was behind her, and secondly because during that particular variation she attained an attitude of licentious imbecility which he fancied.

When the moment arrived, he was very sad. His body and mind working with the skill of a master technician, he savored the depth of his emotions. In order to accomplish his aim he would, in effect, be killing the lovely woman now groaning under him.

"But, in a sense," he rationalized, "I am doing her an honor. She would have died one day anyway, aged and infirm, her body a mass of sagging wrinkles. This way, I freeze her at the height of her beauty, and in the process make her immortal." It reminded him of the fact that the samurai chose the cherry blossom as their symbol because, unlike other flowers, it falls from the branch in the fullness of its fragrance, sacrificing itself so that others might know its precious scent.

It was with mixed feelings that he pressed the needle to the base of her skull, just as she tilted her pelvis backwards to impale her buttocks on his thick cock. He slid into her, causing her to gasp, and at the moment he was imbedded completely between her cheeks, and the look of unutterable pleasure that he was seeking moved across her face, he injected the potion into her skin.

At once she was completely paralyzed. Even her heart stopped mid-beat. For an instant he was breathless at the transformation. She had become a statue. He pulled out slowly, his cock feeling as though it were stuck in a piston tube packed with axle grease. He knelt next to her and turned her over. He could scarcely believe his eyes.

She had been caught at the edge of becoming. Her face was a map of demon lust. As he gazed into her fixed stare, he had trouble convincing himself that she was dead, for even the glint of passion had been captured. For a few seconds he was chilled by the notion that she was still alive, imprisoned in that rigid coffin of flesh.

"But that's absurd," he said, as he went to get a saw.

It was not difficult to sever the head from the body, which he was not really interested in except as a curiosity. It was fascinating to observe that the entire inside of her cunt was flexed in an orgasmic spasm. He put the torso in the bathtub, where another brew of specially prepared chemicals neatly dissolved it.

He brought the head to a special laminating machine he had devised, and placed it in a hollow, where a fine electron mist covered it completely. It sealed the woman in a very delicate plastic, as securely as if she was a driver's license. When he took her out, she looked like a woman about to come, except that she had no body.

"You are mine forever," he whispered, "the real you, the true you, the you that lives eternally in beauty."

After that, his collection grew steadily. He became a regular at most of the singles' bars on the upper east side, and each evening he left with yet another candidate for immortality. Most failed to meet his increasingly exacting standards. Only the best were considered for his hall of fame.

He became adept at discerning types amidst the confusing superficial appearances. With no research ever having been done in the area, he had to construct his own system of classification, a Linnaeus of the rapturous expression. He divided women in scores of ways, such as the various degrees of opening between their lips at certain crucial check points; whether they kept their eyes open or closed, whether or not their nostrils flared. The quality of the eyes was a world of exploration in itself, and he was able to distinguish fifty-three distinct shades of cheek coloration.

His most frequent mistake in the beginning, when he was still exuberant over his success, was to confuse the excitement of fucking with the nature of the expression produced. Some fucked so well that he forgot to watch closely enough. The best fuckers were not always the best lookers, and vice versa.

When he found one that seemed promising, he would not take her all the way on the first night, knowing that the longer he cultivated her, the more sublime would be her expression when she finally did let go. He would nurse her the way a gardener will care for young shoots. The ones who were fortunate enough, or unfortunate enough, to fail to meet his criteria, were shooed out the next day, unceremoniously, so they would know not to try to come back.

Each morning, as he sipped his morning coffee, he would stroll among his heads, kept in a room empty of everything except the pedestals they rested on, and talk to them. He would look from expression of unbearable bliss to expression of deeply tormented joy to expression of total giving, and say, "Well, I had hoped to have another friend for you girls to chat with, but she didn't turn out. For a while there, when she put her ankles around my neck, I thought she might produce a really fine expression, but she was too jaded for me to reach her. An airline stewardess. She later told me she had once been fucked by a mule in a Mexican stag bar. Her face barely lost its composure all night." Or, on those days when he had captured another woman, would proudly carry the head in and say, "This is Frances. Isn't she exquisite?"

And then would light a cigarette and say, "Well, another try tonight," and go up to each one and kiss her full on the mouth, whispering endearments, murmuring, "Remember the night you made it all the way, how good it felt, how close we were?" And then would put out the light and go to work.

His doom was nicely ironic. As he injected a Balinese Temple

Dancer who was part of a troupe visiting the city, her cunt contracted in an esoteric convulsion known only to a few initiates of the cult she had been trained in. His cock was gripped in an unbreakable grasp that was meant to last for no more than a split-second and provide a totally unique sensation. But frozen as she was, he was trapped inside her, a paralyzing spasm of pleasure-pain coursing through his body.

He tried for over an hour to extricate himself, when he realized that gangrene was setting in. He saw the implications fully. To seek medical help would mean being charged with murder, for questions would be asked, his apartment would be searched.

He decided not to prolong the agony. He lifted her up and carried her into the room of heads. He took all his women down, one by one, and put them in a circle on the floor. He lay down in the middle, the woman of the night still in his arms. For a long time he looked from face to face, remembering, weeping. And when his heart was full, he took the instrument he had used on all of them and plunged it into his chest.

He died as he had lived, a slave to the beauty of women.

The Sicilian's Revenge

At fifty-five, there were few pleasures left to him. He enjoyed sleeping, he enjoyed drinking wine and talking with his friends, and he enjoyed renting young Irish prostitutes and having them take their clothes off before him as he watched, his eyes sardonically drinking in their flesh, knowing that they found him repulsive, and then directing them to kneel between his thighs and suck his thick cock until he came, usually not for at least an hour, all the while telling them stories of his childhood in Italy, and when they were finished, dismissing them abruptly. He never had any girl more than once; after he had seen a woman's ass, he lost all further interest in her.

On this day he was in a particularly pensive mood, almost philosophical, as the whore dutifully slavered over his cock. He had just concluded a fairly complex deal which involved the takeover of the Chase Manhattan Bank and all the Rockefeller oil refineries in New Jersey through his company, The Capa Tosta Concrete Corporation. From his offices on the hundred and tenth floor of the World Trade Center Building, he looked down over the grimy expanse of New York City.

His eyes narrowed when they rested on Central Park, Prospect Park, and all the other small sections where nature still had some small toehold. He estimated that he had twenty-five years of vigorous health left, and in that time would not rest until every square inch of the city was covered with cement. Until all five boroughs were drowned in buildings.

His gaze went west. There was still the rest of the United States. But that would have to be for his sons. For himself, he would be content if the city became a single giant mausoleum, a final testimony to his power. It would be a feat such as would make the pyramids of the Pharaohs pale into insignificance.

He patted the head of the girl sucking his cock. "You know, Irish," he said, "all those people down there, they are children. They are fools. Even the educated ones." He paused a moment and added, "Especially the educated ones. They don't know what's real."

His eyes grew watery and dim. "When I was a boy in Italy," he told her, his voice thin, its rhythms moving in cadence to her bobbing head, "we never had all this shit. Dirty air, filthy water, traffic jams, people unhappy all the time. We laughed and we fought. We sang songs and ate fresh fish. We had figs growing in the back yard and I drank fresh goat's milk for breakfast. We lived near the sea, and in those days the sea was clean, the water sparkled. We swam every afternoon. And then there was the wine, and the bread fresh from the oven, and the stars at night, and making love in the hay. Oh, what a time that was! Every week we celebrated the birthday of some saint, and we even had a priest to remind us that there are higher things in the world than man. It wasn't like this pig pen, where the people roll around in garbage and think they are the kings of creation."

He sighed and gave himself over to the sensations produced by the friction of her delicate tongue around the tip of his cock. She swept forward and took the rod into her throat, held it until she gagged, and pulled back. There was something about the old man's calm, his quiet voice, which pacified her, nullified her initial feeling of distaste. The thing in her mouth was iron-hard, and gnarled like a De Nobili cigar. Sucking it was like sucking her thumb when she was a child; it was relaxing, easy, with the single difference that this experience was raked by spasms of such tingling sexuality that her toes curled. Despite her desire to remain detached, she had found herself blowing him with mounting excitement.

"But my stupid mother," he went on, "may the devil stick hot pitchforks in her ass, wanted to go to America. 'The streets are paved with gold,' she kept saying, until my poor father finally gave in, sold the farm, and moved us all here. There was no gold. Just misery, and poverty, and filth. And even if there had been gold, what good would it have been? You can't eat gold, it won't keep you warm at night, it has no love."

He beat his fist against the arm of the chair he was sitting in. "That's what's wrong with this country," he shouted, "there is no love here."

He put his hands on her hair. "Lick it at the tip," he said, and for a few moments he did nothing but watch as she lapped the glistening tool, and payed attention to the fluctuations of pleasure brought by each movement of her tongue.

"But an animal learns to survive wherever it is," he said after a while. "My father bought a grocery store, and we started a new life. It wasn't long before we were paid a visit by the Honored Society, and when I compared their methods of doing business and their success to my father's way of life, well, the choice was obvious. There's no point trying to be honest in the city; it's all based on lies anyway. I became a member of the Family, and today I am don of all the dons."

It struck the girl for the first time that the man whose cock she was sucking was perhaps the most powerful man she might ever meet. Most of her time was spent with fifteen-dollar-a-throw longshoremen, and while she wasn't destitute, she was far from any real financial comfort. The fact that she had been offered five hundred dollars for a few hours of work was astonishing in itself; that it was being paid by the highest Mafia chief in the country was almost too much for her to assimilate.

She had no way of knowing his reasons for picking her, that when he was nineteen he had been struck with an overpowering infatuation for a blue-eyed auburn-haired Irish girl whose fair skin made his dark Mediterranean blood boil. But when, after much trepidation, he had approached her, she had laughed at him, calling him a "spaghetti-stuffed garlic eater." Of course, he had shot her and thrown her body in the East River, but even that was not compensation enough for his wounded pride, and over a thousand times afterwards, he had had his men scour the entire eastern seaboard for young Irish girls that he could subject to the—to his mind —degrading ritual of cock-sucking.

"The mayor, he thinks he runs the city," the old man continued. "But all he does is prance around and look pretty. Nobody with any real power listens to him. He's somebody to put in front of the television cameras so the cattle think their vote means something. No, it's the ones who control the life systems and the death systems who are in command, only most of them are so stupid, they don't realize it yet.

"Look at the police. Some of the commanders are beginning to figure out that they have thirty-thousand men, armed with hand guns, and with access to machine guns, horses, tear gas, tanks, grenades. But if they made a move, they'd have the state militia to contend with, and the federal government. They'll have to lie low until the whole nation is falling apart in chaos.

"But they are only the most obvious candidates. Think of the firemen who can allow the city to burn, or perhaps even burn it themselves. And the garbage-men, who only strike for higher wages, but could consolidate as a political force, threatening to let plague conditions arise if their demands weren't met. Still, none of these people have any political awareness."

The girl continued sucking. He had put his hands on the back of her head and was guiding her by imparting a momentum to her motions. She let her lips go slack and allowed his cock to bob in and out of her mouth, her tongue licking it each time it entered and each time it left. She had begun to have fantasies that he might want her as his private whore, and drew pictures in her mind of a swank apartment, a complete wardrobe, a sports car, charge accounts, and trips to Puerto Rico in the winter. She dropped her reserve and worked up a feverish pleasure in what she was doing, giving herself up to wanton expressions, hoping he would be taken by the masks of lasciviousness she wore. The old man had seen all of this before.

"And even they don't strike at the heart of things," he went on. "Who controls the drinking water, the water to put out fires? Did you ever give a second thought to all those men you see climbing in and out of sewers? Everybody looks down on them, but no one stops to consider that they have access to switches which control the city's vital fluid. While the mayor makes speeches for the newspapers, grimy men with wrenches hold our destiny in their hands.

"But it doesn't end there. You can almost hear the people

from Con Ed smirking. Do you remember the night of the great blackout? That was just a test to see if it could be done. It was fun for a few hours, but what would happen after a few days and nights without electricity? Suck it, Irish, suck it! No lights anywhere. Traffic snarled because the traffic lights didn't work. Refrigerators useless, food spoiling. No radio, no television, no elevators, no subways. We would be plunged back into the Stone Age in no time. Bands would form. The gun and the knife would be the law. And not too many would survive.

"And there are other possibilities," he said, waving his hand through the air. "Radicals blowing up the bridges, tunnels, subway tracks. Or the telephone company, operating the central nerve cord that runs through all city life. It is the indispensible tool of business, and without it business would fold. And without business, there is no New York."

He was approaching orgasm. The moment of climax was still five minutes away, but he could sense its beginning. With his body as calm as it was, he was able to give himself to sensation without tension, and thus truly savor the long deep swell which preceded ejaculation. Capable of dispensing with any consideration of the girl except as a tool for his pleasure, he could devote his undivided attention to his inner state.

"But not one of them suspects the overwhelmingly obvious truth as to what real power is." His voice held a tremor of excitement, partially from the growing heat in his loins, partially from the imapct of articulating his vision. "And that is with *me*" he continued, "because the one thing they all have to do is *live here*! They must *spend their time here*. And I'm the one who decides what kind of place they get to stay in. No matter who's in command, no matter what form of government, no matter what the state of the economy, the most important reality of the city is its environment. And what makes the environment is the architecture. And I control the architecture."

His voice purred. "I'll make sure there is nothing left but concrete. Mile after mile of living earth has already been covered up, suffocated, and giant stone buildings loom where trees used to grow. There is almost nothing natural left. Most plant life has been destroyed, most animal life, most insect life. The people have nothing left but hard surfaces to walk on, to sit on, to lie on, to look at. Even the sky is hard to see. They are allowed some few cats and dogs and horses, and the pitiful specimens they put in the concrete prisons they call zoos. But that is all. And soon, even they will disappear. The pigeons will be killed. Only rats and roaches will remain. Rats and roaches and people.

"And as they become sicker and sicker, more and more confused and unhappy, they will never begin to guess what their trouble is, that's how unbelievably ignorant they are. They will blame the mayor, they will blame the police chief, they will blame drugs and permissive education. They will revolt, they will change leaders. They will try everything. But the obvious will never occur to them, that they are slowly dying, being killed by the lack of life around them. They will go to their graves as blind as when they were alive. And I shall win. I shall build everywhere. Cement will rule the earth!"

As he said the last words his thighs tensed and a voluminous spurt of sperm burst into the girl's mouth. She went through all the motions of swallowing it as though it were some kind of nectar, hoping to please the old man with her gusto. But the instant after he came he pushed her away, stared into her face for a moment, and shook his head to deny the memory which refused to let him rest.

"Go suck the boys in the back room," he said.

She began to protest, caught up in a swirling disappointment, but a glint in his eyes told her she had better not say a word. She stood up, licked a few drops of semen from her lips, and petulantly walked toward the door, her buttocks jiggling as she went, to the back room where seven men sat around a wide table playing cards. She would be told to crawl under the table, and go from cock to cock until she had done them all, and then be bundled out into the street, a half a thousand dollars and several insights richer.

The old man buttoned his pants and walked to the window. The city was practically invisible because of the thickly polluted air. Even from his great height he could hear the infernal roar, the din of triumphant machinery. Everywhere cars chugged like ancient beasts, spewing gases in their wake, and at a thousand sites the relentless momentum of construction, more and taller buildings rising to occupy even the smallest bit of free space. And through all this the people walked, their ears shattered by the noises, their nostrils pinched against the stench, their entire bodies incessantly punished by the crunch of crystallized finance. Seen from above, the scene resembled nothing so much as a *danse macabre* of zombies, hulks whose souls had long since been sucked dry.

"I will have revenge on you," he muttered, "for fooling my mother that there could be a good life here, for taking my father away from his land and causing him to die in an unheated tenement, away from the sea and the sky, and for forcing me to become such an evil man to survive. I will destroy you, and my children shall destroy your entire nation. Just by giving you what you want, more cement, more concrete, more steel. To cover the beautiful earth, to tear down the forests, to poison the lakes and the rivers.

"And for what? To build these human garbage dumps, these cities. To construct highways and bridges and dams and all the stupid structures that you worship."

He laughed, a horrible creaking sound.

"I will give you what you want, America," he shouted. "I will give you *progress*. And it will take you straight into the mouth of hell."

Circus of Jade

Butch Medusa lay amidst the pile of bodies. There were eleven other women in the heap, the result of the most ambitious project she had yet undertaken. The group contained representatives of each of the world's races, and was a palette of wildly complementary skin colors and hair textures. Both tall and short were there, as well as fat and thin. Each of the women was from one of the sun signs of the Zodiac, and Butch had personally tested and tasted all of them for copiousness and flavor of vaginal secretions. But now, after all the drugs and music, after the hours of flirtation and foreplay, after the weeks of preparation and expectation, as asses and cunts and mouths and breasts and feet rolled and flashed in a continuous panorama of sensuality, Butch had to admit that she was bored.

"This orgy has no socially redeeming value," she said to herself as a lithe Ethiopian sword-dancer sucked one of her nipples between her lips. Loathe as she was to admit it, Butch had come to the end of a cycle and was unwilling to garner the energy to break into a new phase.

She had begun her career one night by sweeping into a lesbian bar dressed in a suit of chain mail and carrying a mace. The place was instantly polarized, the more strident exponents of the new female image finding her intolerably outre, while the lustier women flocked to her side, glad that at least one person was still ready to champion unfashionable stereotypes. For five years subsequent to her coming out, she had run amok in the ultra-sophisticated circles of post-decadent tribadism, imparting a quality of aesthetic ruthlessness to a life style that had been foundering in sterile polemics. Among her vassals were many daughters of the wealthy, and she had no difficulty producing the money she needed to support her rampant metatheatre.

The thought she had been suppressing for months now came to the surface of her consciousness. "To do what I want to do, I really need some cocks."

She blew a whistle and the writhing mass of bodies quivered once and fell still. She lept to her feet, breasts jiggling.

"Sweet Sappho's pussy," she yelled, "is this the best you can manage? If I want choreography I'll find a bunch of fags. I want passion, goddamnit." And reaching behind her, she picked up a fourteen-foot bull whip with which she began to flay the women lying in front of her.

"What do I have to do to get some *feeling* around here?" she shouted, and laid about her with the thick ugly leather instrument.

The cries she extracted, however, were only bleats of pain, and she was no longer interested in mere sadomasochism, having had her fill one afternoon when she flogged three virgins into insensibility on the secluded grounds of a Connecticut estate an admirer had put at her disposal. She threw the whip down in disgust and went to her study to ponder.

"It's not their fault," she thought, "they're doing the best they know how. It's just that there's no sense of purpose." She lit a joint and settled back on her zebra-skin watercouch. Plunging into a deep trance, she found many of the fragments of a vision that had been haunting her coming into place. It was an idea so compelling that she hesitated even to think about it. But she was hungry for challenge, and within an hour knew what she had to do.

"It won't be easy," she mused, "finding the men I need for the job. The gays are free enough, but they don't really want to fuck women. And I have to have both male and female energy for the project. The straights are so crippled I couldn't even put an honest proposition to most of them. Aren't there any lovers left? Men who are pliable enough to take orders from a woman one moment and then throw her down and rip off a piece of ass the next? I need men with firm bodies and warm hearts, men with hard cocks and clear minds, men with fire in their blood and mercury in their egos. Where will I find them?"

The next day began a quest which was to take her over the entire nation and last for almost two years. She put her affairs in order and left a skeleton crew behind to answer her mail and maintain her Park Avenue duplex. And then she began her search.

The technique she used was simple. Whenever she saw a man she sensed was ripe for plucking, she would walk up to him and say, clearly and directly, "Would you like to fuck me?"

If he answered too quickly or was thrown into confusion, she abandoned him at once. She wouldn't consider any man who wasn't together enough to assimilate her approach instantaneously, take a moment to breathe and look at her, peer into her eyes and appraise her body, and respond from the core of some real impulse.

Those who passed the first screening were taken to her hotel room and allowed to fuck her. And as the man went through his motions, she registered impressions of his total being. If, at the end of the first fuck, she still thought he had potential, she would outline her scheme and offer him room and board to work with her. After she had hired her first helper, of course, the game became trickier, for the ensuing prospects would be confronted not only with a woman's asking him what no other woman had probably ever asked before, never so honestly and openly, but also with the man standing next to her.

At the end of three months she had found four men.

The movement began to grow interesting as a spirit of camaraderie seized the group. It was the first time Butch had seen America and was amazed at how much of it was still unspoiled by urbanization. In Santa Fe she picked up a deaf mute, and she took her band into the surrounding hills for a retreat.

That night Butch found herself lying naked on her back, bent over a bedroll, as the men played poker and drank coffee around a fire. Every once in a while one of them would stroll over to fuck her. For her part, it was pleasant to enjoy the cool night air and look at the stars, letting her mind drift, to have her revery interrupted only by the sweet penetration of a cock or by a mouth on one of her breasts or by a hand under her buttocks.

The men, on their part, enjoyed a kind of friendship almost impossible for men to know any longer. Free from financial worries, they could allow themselves to relax. With a woman they could fuck at any time they wanted, they were liberated from sexual tension. And since they all shared the same woman under the same conditions, they had no cause for jealousy, and the bond among them grew unhampered. And it was just the strength of the bond that Butch relied upon for the realization of her vision.

At the end of a year she had gathered seventeen men and returned to the city. The power of their circle was enormous and she was ready to try the next level of operations. She got back in late August, a month before the beginning of the New York season, and started her preparations at once.

First came the costuming. The men were all dressed a like, with short leather skirts, gold earrings in their right ears, and jade bracelets on their left wrists. She led esoteric psychophysical exercises and dances to coordinate their reflexes and cement their sense of unity. She gave lectures to pinpoint her objective. During that period they were allowed no sex so their lust would build.

And when they were at a fine edge, she brought in a victim for them to practice on, a nineteen year old debutante, slim, auburn haired, with only handful of fucks in her experience and a literary infatuation with lesbian love. Butch picked her up at one of the consciousness-raising sessions that have superseded bars as cruising grounds, ravished her for an entire night, and primed her for the experience of being had by a band of men. Half hypnotized, half yearning to live out a fantasy she had been barely able to admit to herself, she agreed to cooperate.

"It's a shame to have to destroy her," Butch thought, "but the men have to be forged into a seamless unit, and only a ritual murder will really do the trick. Besides, once she is really opened up, it would be impossible for her to live in the world anyway."

The night of the affair, after the girl was fucked for the fifty-third time, the last edge of her resistance to madness cracked, and for the next five hours she screamed herself hoarse, pleading for more. "Fuck me, fuck me, fuck me," she shouted over and over again, a hundred times, a thousand times, ten thousand times, the skin of inhibition totally torn and the well of her inexhaustible sexuality yielding its waters.

Finally, Butch dispatched her cleanly, a single bullet through the temple, snuffing out the torment that had its roots in ecstasy, in the eternal restlessness of the flesh.

"This is the power we are going to tap," Butch told the men who looked at the corpse with wide eyes. "We have just begun to unleash the limitless force of sexual energy. When we can control that force and harness the power of the orgasm, we will have a weapon which will reduce all the atomic stockpiles on Earth to the status of toys. And then we shall impose peace on the world. But first, we have to get rid of the body."

Butch called on her reserve army of women, and found an equal number to match the men. There was another month of intense preparation, and then she was ready for her first test: the formation of a sexual cyclotron.

The women all knelt in a circle, their asses up and away from the center, while the men crouched behind them, their cocks at the openings of the cunts. Butch lay in the center, her head pointing north. At her signal, the men all entered the women at once, and began fucking with slow regular strokes. The women held hands all around, as did the men, so that from above, at a Busby Berkeley angle, the whole thing looked like a jellyfish pulsating at the edges. And at the brain of the superorganism was Butch Medusa, coursing all the vibrations through herself. The rhythm increased as a group consciousness began to form. Everyone was aware of the state of everyone else's being.

Gradually, control shifted from the individuals to the group as a whole. A power emerged that was greater than the ability of any single person to claim. It began to take over by itself, reducing the men and women to units in a conglomerate. Unity was achieved through adherence to the dictates of the over-soul.

Orgasm approached, a single orgasm which included the bodies of everyone in the circle. The men joined through their arms, the women joined through their hands, the men and women joined through cock and cunt, all eyes on the body in the center, all minds empty of thoughts, and Butch gathering all the energy in a single sustained awareness, they came together. And at that instant, Butch was buoyed by a sheet of blue light and lifted six feet off the floor. She hovered for eight minutes and then drifted slowly back down to the rug.

For that period of time, through the city, all hostility in every human being was allayed. Policemen stopped with their fingers on the trigger, husbands and wives stopped mid-argument, taxi drivers stopped with curses on their lips. Not one violent act was commited. Everyone was enveloped in a euphoric cloud, and for weeks afterwards scientists speculated as to whether some electronic mass hysteria was the cause. Many found grounds to reaffirm their faith in God. Some claimed that extraterrestrial beings were influencing the earth.

The group was giddy with success, but Butch calmed them down. "We can't go too fast," she warned. "Too much joy all at once would destroy the fabric of every civilization in the world. People would revert to their simple animal state. Governments would collapse. And the havoc that followed would mean the death of millions. Let them get used to happiness little by little. And meanwhile, we can increase our numbers. One day we'll be able to sustain the effect indefinitely, and then we can open all the switches and fuck the species into survival."

The plan might have worked except for an unforeseen event. Butch Medusa fell in love. She met a man who filled her with all the inane and irresistible feeling such as used to propel teenagers into romantic raptures. The rational part of her realized that to give in to her emotions would destroy the final chance humanity might have to keep from going over the brink into total ruin. But she was helpless before the mood of surrender.

"It's what I get for fooling around with all those cocks," she said to herself bitterly. "Such a fate would never have befallen me if I had stayed a lesbian. This is what I get for trying to do good."

The man was not the kind who would tolerate her unbridled promiscuity, so she abandoned her commune. She moved to Long Island, where he worked as a professor of sociology at Stony

Brook College. She had three children and spent her days at war with herself, hating the fact that she really enjoyed her new situation. She never spoke of her past even when the women in her bridge club began to talk about sex, revealing their fantasies and infidelities. Everyone thought her a model wife, which indeed she was.

The people in the duplex, without the unifying power of her vision, soon degenerated into a crowd of rowdy low-level orgiasts. The neighbors started to complain, and one night the place was raided. They were all booked on charges of indecent behavior, given suspended sentences, and told to leave the city. The body of the girl who had been shot had been smuggled out and buried on Staten Island, and thus was never found. The human race continued in its erratic stumbling toward oblivion.

Bowel Boogie

Only her body was tied down; she could still move her head and look around the room.

It was ten feet high by ten feet wide by ten feet long. It was constructed entirely of tile. There was a vent in the ceiling to let in air, and a vent in the floor to let water drain out. A spout jutted from one wall, and over it was a shelf with various instruments.

She was chained to a table built of soft stone, held utterly immobile. Her wrists were manacled at her sides, a steel band went over her waist, and her feet were fastened to raised stirrups so that her legs were lifted and spread apart. She took a deep breath and closed her eyes.

The door opened slowly, a thick wooden partition with soundproof slats cemented to both sides. The doctor stepped in. He was one of the world's foremost therapists, having written a book called *The Secondary Stutter*, in which he traced all neurosis to the suppression of embarrassment people feel when farting. He closed the door behind him and beamed on the woman.

"Well, Ms. Schneider," he said in a booming voice, "how good to meet you."

She looked up and gasped. The man wore hip boots, a long raincoat, and rubber gloves. His face was covered with a black mask. She had been told that he would want to remain anonymous, but it hadn't occurred to her that he would hide more than his name. The social worker at the clinic she had applied to for psychotherapy had explained that she might partake of an experimental program without charge, and in addition to having her difficulties cleared up, would be helping the march of science in its striving to obliterate all mental illness.

She was told that the treatment would have to remain secret and that she would not know who would be treating her, in order to protect him from lawsuits. Ms. Schneider had had her doubts, but she felt in desperate need of help, and couldn't afford to pay for it, so she agreed.

He walked over to the table. "Before we begin," he said, his voice deep and reassuring. "I'm sure you will have a few questions. But first I'd like to tell you a little about what we'll be doing."

The woman shifted her weight and he glanced at her through the narrow slits of his disguise. She was thirty-nine, worked as an elementary school teacher, and had never been married. Her body was slim, the flesh still firm. Uneventful legs blossomed into arched buttocks, and small breasts nicely graced her upper chest. Her pubic hair was sparse and her outer cunt lips were folded against each other like hands clasped in prayer.

"To put it most directly," he began, "my work is not a departure from, but the most recent development of, the psychoanalytic discoveries of Sigmund Freud. You've heard of Freud? The orthodox analysts would have me tarred and feathered if they knew what I was doing, but mostly because they are afraid to face the logical conclusions of their own theories. That is why I must say nothing about my work until I can prove that my technique is effective."

The woman opened her mouth to speak but he cut in before she could say a word. "Although I subsume the work of all the men and women who have gone before me, my approach is original, a totally new synthesis. And beyond the theoretical correctness is the fact that my technique is *absolute*." His voice rang with a strange vibration, sounding hollow beneath the mask. "You see, that has been the problem. All the great minds have understood neurosis and formulated their theories, but none of them could come up with a cure that would work in all cases. And this is to be my immortal contribution. The infallible cure for all psychopathic disturbances."

He began pacing, but since the room was so small and the table took up the central space, he was forced to walk in a circle around the woman's body. She attempted to follow him with her eyes as he prowled. "The discovery of my technique, as with that of penicillin, was accidental. All the elements were present, and I just happened to be there to put them together. I remember the afternoon well. I had just finished reading the passage in *Function of the Orgasm* where Reich describes his basic insight into masochism. He found that what the masochist really seeks is the feeling of bursting open, of having his energy flow outward, through his armored self. The masochist doesn't enjoy pain itself, but hopes to find a release in pain.

"That was on my mind when I opened my mail and found a brochure from the Eulenspiegel Society, an organization composed of sadists and masochists dedicated to erasing prejudices about their condition. I was struck by the way in which life is always struggling to express itself in a positive fashion, even when it passes through what must seem like terrible aberrations.

"It was just then that I felt the first peristaltic wave that signals a bowel movement. I went into the bathroom, closing the door behind me. As I turned the knob, however, I realized that there was no one else in the house! I was thunderstruck. My shame at such a basic biological activity was so deep that it led me to the most absurd behavior, closing the door against the censure of society when no other member of society was even present. I sat down and my eyes moved idly across the wall opposite and fell upon my wife's douche bag which hung from a hook. I don't know how to describe that moment. Choirs sang, and the room filled with light. It all came together in a crescendo of truth."

He stopped pacing and grabbed one of the woman's ankles tightly. "Do you see?" he said, his voice brimming with emotion. "Does it begin to make sense now?"

The woman thought he was stark raving mad. She did what people in rising panic often do, and reached into the recent past to recall the last moments of normality she could remember. The clinic was a highly respected institution, so when the nurse had asked her to remove her clothing and had fastened her to the table, there was still some sense of being connected to the workaday world, even though the trappings were bizarre. Ms. Schneider had a fully conditioned faith in public organizations, and she drew on that to counter the brunt of her perception:

that she was helpless in a locked room with a maniac peering down at her naked body.

"I don't think I want to continue with this," she bleated.

"Ah ha!" he shouted. "That's the point. Very few people do. All other therapies have failed simply because at the point of greatest resistance the therapist allowed the patient to leave. I will change all that. My vision demands it. People must be saved in spite of themselves. That's the whole issue with neurosis. And nothing except my technique has any chance of curing neurosis, and of ultimately saving the world. Nothing else includes all the necessary elements. Bringing forth childhood repressions, it will allow that feeling of bursting so you will stop shrinking from life, and it will put you in touch with your need and your pain. It will allow you your full range of expression, and plumb to the core of your sexual nature. It will attack your most deep-seated inhibition, the one which grows from the cornerstone contribution of our civilization to the world: early toilet training."

The woman started to protest that none of this seemed connected to the relatively uncomplicated problems she had been dealing with, but he seemed to read her mind. "Your unhappiness is felt by you in one way, but its causes are beyond your awareness. You will see. You will fight me because I will show you your true self. You will scream, you will hate, you will cry, you will yearn, you will surrender, and you will win. You will have a total experience and for the first time in your life you will come alive. And nothing or no one will prevent you from achieving your goal, least of all yourself. I won't let you stop yourself from becoming healthy. I will force the neurosis out of you."

He reached to the shelf behind him and picked up a long hose with a plastic nozzle. "Ms. Schneider," he said, "you have the honor to be the first patient to try the most revolutionary treatment in the history of psychology: Enema Therapy."

The woman sobbed openly. She could not believe that she had allowed things to go so far, that she hadn't stopped when she saw the room, or when the nurse tied her to the table.

"I don't want to," she cried out to the doctor.

"Of course you don't," he said cheerfully, attaching the hose to the spigot on the wall. "At least, the superficial part of you doesn't. But the deeper part, the part that brought you to seek help in the first place, is calling for help, and help it shall get."

He brought the nozzle level with the table top. He fingered some Vaseline from a jar on the shelf and delicately applied it to the woman's anus.

"No," she keened, now almost totally out of control.

"You'll see, you'll see," he crooned.

He placed the nozzle between her clenched buttocks and gently pushed, inserting it fully into her body. She tried to squirm away but was held too tightly. Her thighs bulged with tension. The doctor stepped back and viewed his handiwork.

"No matter what happens," he said, "just remember one thing: no physical harm can come to you here. Your own worse enemy is tied securely to the table. You may go insane for a while, but that's the only way to reach true sanity. There can be no reconstitution without regression, that's my motto."

He reached behind him and, taking a few seconds to appreciate the historic import of the moment, he turned the handle, beginning the flow of water into Ms. Schneider's ass.

She filled up for almost twenty minutes. As the hot fluid entered her, she began to howl. Again and again she reached a point where she thought she could take no more and begged him to stop, but he was implacable. "It's all been measured ahead of time," he would say. Pain enveloped her in waves, giving way to a peculiar kind of pleasure, a sort of tingling release. She tried to back away from the nozzle, but her body was fixed in place. The doctor got an erection, watching her thrash about, her cunt winking lewdly above the phallic nozzle, but he maintained professional discipline and his stiff cock did not show beneath the heavy raincoat.

He maintained stoic composure. Even when she seemed on the brink of collapse, ready to faint or actually pass away, he never lost the necessary faith in his treatment. She was like a film shown by a beserk projector, her body threatening to burst as it yielded thousands upon thousands of repressed memories and feelings and thoughts locked in her muscles and brain cells. It was like a seven year analysis gone through at the speed of sound, and with total abreaction. Her frame shuddered like a test plane in a wind tunnel. And she reached a state of such complete energy expansion that her hair stood on end, rising two feet from her scalp.

Finally, he turned the water off. It had begun to seep out around the edges of the nozzle and he knew that she was filled to the brim. When she felt the stoppage of flow, there was a momentary relief, but with astounding swiftness he pulled the nozzle out and stuck in a stopper, corking her as neatly as a wine bottle.

"Oh God," she wailed.

"We are going to remain like this for a little while," he said. "The first phase is over, and you have survived the initial trauma. Now the real work begins, for you will no longer be able to hide behind your freneticism and hysteria. In this treatment, all the masks of defense must be stripped and you must face your actual condition. We must go on until you are literally incapable of sustaining your experience, and your mind shatters with trying to rationalize it all. Then the unconscious will be liberated and the basic structural changes can take place in your character."

The following five hours were chaotic. She became feverish and then snapped into lucidity. She fell asleep and had bloated dreams. She babbled out loud. She tried again and again to expel the cork and push out the fluid, but was thrown back into helplessness. She entered the death state. For a while, she was raked with erotic flashes, and at one point began to grind her hips up toward the ceiling, running her tongue over her lips and moaning until she had an orgasm.

Occasionally the doctor added more water to replace what had been absorbed through the colon. Some of the sounds that ripped from her throat would have melted the heart of Satan himself, but the therapist was unshakeable.

"I must help her see it through," he said to himself. A lifetime of work was culminating in this experiment, and not only his reputation but his deepest definition of self was at stake. He hated neurosis the way a saint hates sin. His hope to rescue the world from destruction was wild enough to tax the limits of his rational mind, but some more primitive center within him goaded him on.

"The enema," he thought, "our only hope is in the enema."

He watched, waiting for the sign that the treatment was complete. He did not know what form it would take, but had unmoveable faith that she would come out the other side of her heightened anguish and go on into a life of freedom. All the while she seemed to be in the throes of unbearable suffering, radical internal changes were taking place, and he could do nothing but wait.

Finally, a profound shudder went through her. She had come to the end of her metamorphosis. Her soul had been scrubbed clean and brought to its basic grain. She was utterly naked. A lifetime of overlay had loosened and now floated inside her. Her characterological tensions had been dissolved and there was no portion of her mind which was any longer unknown to her.

"I've done it," he whispered, "I've accomplished in a few hours what therapists take years to do. She is cured. I can see it."

At that instant, the woman let out a wail that was indistinguishable from the cry a baby lets out right after birth.

"Love," the woman said, "I want love."

The doctor's eyes stung with tears. The woman had contacted the core of her being and been reborn. His approach was vindicated. He took a deep breath, and with a sweeping gesture, he pulled the plug.

She gushed for an eternity. Jet after jet of water burst from her. She vibrated with the release of all her sickness, the literal and metaphoric shit she had been keeping inside her. The brown fluid splashed on the walls over the floor, ran down the therapist's raincoat, poured down the drain.

"Free," he shouted, "you are free," and turned on the spigot again, this time to play the hose in a stream over her body as he undid her locks and chains. She sprang up from the table, pulsing with the river of new life that filled her, with the cosmic energy that was once more a part of her heritage. He put down the hose and the woman stood in front of him, her face radiant with happiness, a blue aura shining around her head.

"I don't know what to say," she said, "everything is . . . different now."

"I understand," he replied.

"I didn't realize how afraid I was. Not only on the table, but for my whole life. Afraid of everyone and everything. Why, I even used to be afraid to cross the street!"

She got dressed and the two of them talked in his office for a while. After removing his mask he proved to be a pleasant-looking man in his early fifties.

"Come back tomorrow," he said. "I want to take some psychological tests and tape your account of your experience. I'm going to present this to the world."

After she left, as he sat in silent enjoyment of his accomplishment, he heard a screech outside his window, followed by a hubbub of voices. Crossing the street bravely, the woman had been hit by a bus and was killed instantly. He rushed out. As he stood over her body a small tic developed at the edge of his mouth.

"It's always more complicated than one thinks," he muttered as he went back inside the clinic where he sat at his desk and began scribbling furiously in his notebook.

Yesterday's Lago

Neither could remember how or where they met; they assumed it had been at a party. But suddenly, they were friends, and from the first shared an intimacy and trust which went deeper than anything they knew with anyone else, including their mates.

They experienced that rare and precious gift of total communion. They could sit for hours, holding hands, speaking or not speaking, attuned to a communication which went from words to silence and back to words without an interruption in the flow of meaning. Unaware of themselves, they often struck classic postures, and one might find them lost in one another's eyes, their fingers intertwined, sighing openly.

Albert was a poet, and chained to his dry despair. The wife and two children who inhabited his days seemed something of an afterthought, a footnote to his central concern. He held a job to support his family, and went through the motions of relationship, but it was only when he was alone, a beam of light transforming his desk top into a stage as he hunched against the glare of the white sheet of paper that challenged him, his hand holding a sharpened pencil hovering like a hawk about to strike, that he felt whole.

Until he met Margaret.

"You are as real to me as poetry," he told her, and she wept with the joy of recognition.

Through the years they came to comfort one another in times of crisis, to celebrate in times of plenitude. At first they attempted to integrate the singularity of their bond into their wider social contexts, but both her husband and his wife began to seethe with jealousy even though the two of them had not know so much as a kiss by way of sexual contact.

"I'd almost prefer it if you fucked her," his wife told him, "then you'd stop idealizing her and imagining that she's all that different from me."

Margaret's husband left her, and Albert began to visit her at her apartment regularly, lying to his wife about where he was. "It's strange," he said to Margaret, "you're like my sister, and I have to sneak off to see you."

At first they spoke mostly of her marriage, her suffering. Albert was a mountain of support, listening, guiding, caring. And leaning on him, she was able to effect the difficult transition from knowing herself only through the reflection of another to having a sense of identity as a single woman.

And as that took place, of course, she began to feel her need for a man once more, but this time promising herself that she would not allow herself to be vulnerable, but would take what a man had to offer by way of completion, and give back as good as she got. For her deeper aspects, she had Albert.

In this mood, her encounters with men began to take on an odd twist, for she discovered that she hungered for bad treatment. Her husband had known how to be mentally and emotionally cruel to her, and it was, in fact, his disgust for himself for falling into that trap which had prompted his leaving; but she could not find the same sort of punishment with men who were essentially one-night stands. A shift took place, subtle at first, but with rapid acceleration into clearly defined forms, until she recognized her craving for physical pain.

She didn't want to tell Albert, for fear she would repulse him, but one night she could hold it back no longer.

"I think I'm a masochist," she said.

"You've always been," he told her. "We've talked about that before."

"It's different now," she said. "It used to be passive and unconscious, but now I'm an active masochist. I openly ask for it."

She told him about the previous night. She had been sitting at home, knitting and listening to music, when a great restlessness seized her. Her legs trembled and she found her heart beating quickly. She went out into the street like a zombie, heading for the nearest bar. It wasn't too long before a man sat next to her, a grizzled dockworker in his mid-forties who loooked as though he had been drinking steadily for the past thirty years. His very gruesomeness sent shivers of contorted desire through her, and while he was not cerebrally capable of formulating and articulating the nuances of the situation, his animal intelligence understood at once what was going on.

He grabbed her arm and led her out into the night. By that time she was quivering in anticipation and could barely stand. She dimly remembered lurching through obscure neighborhoods, and being half carried up a flight of stairs to his room. He flung her down on the bed and leapt up next to her. For a few moments he was pure frenzy, all the frustration of his lifetime pouring out on the willing woman who had given herself up to be used. He slapped and pawed and bunched her up, flinging her back and forth like a half-empty sack of flour. She could recall none of the details, only being aware that he might kill her, and not caring for anything except the brute energy that erupted from him.

"That's what I remember most clearly," she told Albert, "that I was sucking his energy from him, and I would do anything for that energy, even to letting him beat me."

"What happened then?" Albert asked, his voice calm and gentle, his mien serene, his attitude one of total compassion and acceptance.

"He ripped my clothes off," she continued. "And then it was sheer jungle sex. He had a cock like a policeman's billy, and he used it the same way, to beat me with. He didn't know what to do first, and he kept tossing me around in a dozen different ways, fucking me in the mouth, in the cunt, in the ass. All the while he kept slapping me and calling me the most foul names. And I . . . well, I enjoyed it so much it scared me. I just kept shouting, 'Yes, yes, this is what I want, this is what I've always wanted.'"

She paused. "When he came, I dug my nails a half inch into his skin and he didn't even feel it. Afterwards we were both a little flabbergasted, and when I was leaving he said, 'I'm going to make believe this was a dream, because this isn't going to happen to me again, and I don't want to start wanting it, because you aren't going to want me another time. Your type, you'll do this a thousand times with a thousand different men before you're through.' And I knew he was right. He was so dumb and sweet and sad that I got carried away and I went down on my knees and gave him a long, slow blow job. And I loved it. Being in that tawdry apartment sucking that stranger's cock after he had practically torn me apart."

She looked up. "What do you think, Albert? Am I sick?"

He stroked her hair and held her head in his hands and gazed deeply into her liquid eyes.

"I've only had one criterion in my life," he told her. "Anything which can be seen as poetry is its own justification. If you view it as something ugly, then that's what it becomes. If you can sing its beauty, then that is all there is. And your soul is the soul of poetry. If you remember that, you are free to do things which would horrify the timid and the trite."

Then he smiled, and added, "But none of that should let you forget that one time you might meet up with someone whose frustrations lie deeper than your dockworker's, and you could very well end up tied to a bed while some maniac tattoos your body with a razor blade. Or even less dramatically, but more probably, that same man loses his sense of proportion and smashes a fist into your mouth relieving you of a dozen teeth." He frowned, lit a cigarette, and went on, "But the real danger is more insidious. The body builds a tolerance for any sort of sensation, and if you take this path, you will start to need more and more violent behavior to achieve the same levels of stimulation. It's like heroin or any other drug."

She lay with her head against his chest and wept silently. "You are such a beautiful person and such a dear, dear friend," she said. "You care so much for me, and yet you leave me absolutely free. You never censor or blame."

"How could it be otherwise?" he replied.

The more lurid of the possibilities didn't come to pass, but the last one did. While Margaret didn't fall into the hands of a madman or receive any scars or permanent damage, she did enter an escalating cycle of sadomasochistic activity. Like so many in that particular endgame, she learned the value of choreography and expertise. She came to prefer a man who knew how to use a whip with discretion and skill over someone who struck out blindly and in rage.

In time she was introduced among a number of the formal and informal circles composed of people who shared similar tastes. She was initiated into more delicate forms of torture, including the judicious use of hot wax, the proper placement of needles, the hanging bar and nipple clips. She once spent a weekend as slave to an entire household, being used and abused by almost twenty men and women for three days. And, in logical progression, she developed a taste for what were called, in that clique, water games.

"It was extraordinary, Albert," she said. "There I was, my hands tied behind me, having just been fucked by three men at once, kneeling in front of a fourth. He told me to open my mouth and I thought he wanted me to suck his cock. But when I took it, it wasn't hard. The upper part of my face was covered with a leather mask, so I didn't know what was coming. Then this incredible sensation, a stream of hot liquid on my tongue. I still didn't know, and then the taste hit me. A fantastic taste, pungent and sweet and bitter and salty all at once. And then I knew. He was pissing in my mouth! And it drove me wild. I reached up and put his whole cock inside me and let him piss down my throat. And all the while my knees were shaking and I almost climaxed with excitement."

She looked at him, wondering whether this outrage would perturb him at all. Telling him was a treat, for she was able to experience her episodes at another level, but from time to time she became afraid of alienating his affection. But he only nodded and said, "Unless the person has some disease, urine is perfectly sterile. It can't hurt you. In fact, it's probably safer then the city's drinking water."

"Have you ever done anything like that?" she asked.

"I'm afraid my sexual tastes have always been suffocatingly pedestrian," he told her.

They continued in that manner for more than a year, and one night he arrived looking drawn. She tried to cheer him up with wine and stories of her week's activity but he became more and more glum. Finally he blurted out, "Susan left me. She's taken the children."

For the first time in their long relationship, she listened more to him than he to her. And after long, long hours of his pouring himself out, exposing a weakness and sensibility to pain that he had never shown before, at four in the morning, exhausted, he asked, "Do you mind if I stay here a day or two? I don't want to face that empty apartment just yet."

The two days stretched into four, and the four into a week, and finally he left. It was as though he didn't want to go, and yet felt extremely awkward staying longer. Her heart went out to him. After so many years, she had a chance to help him, to provide succor for his hurt.

But he did not call her for several weeks, and she could not reach him on the phone. Finally, she went to his apartment, and found him drunk and disheveled, the place a shambles. She got him to shower and shave, cleaned the house, and made a huge dinner for him. Later, they sat on the couch and talked. It was the first time that she knew him without his having his wife, and the difference was palpable.

During a deep silence, something totally unforeseen happened. He held her to him, as he so often had, but this time his arms tightened until her face tilted up, and his lips covered hers in a kiss that transmitted an unmistakable urgency.

Something profoundly deep within her melted. The transcendent liberty she had discovered in her body blended with the hunger in her heart, and in an instant she surrendered totally to him, on fire with that unique melange of physical desire, emotional need, and intellectual affinity to which is given the name love.

Instantly they were one, and without a thought they launched themselves into a total lovemaking which thundered with the force of so many years of waiting and building. The form was completely constructed, their friendship was absolute, she could give herself, give herself rapturously, having the abandon she had known in her body with others and the fullness she had felt in her heart for Albert. Now they were one, and it seemed as though her entire life had been a preparation for this moment.

The next morning they decided to live together, and they moved to a new neighborhood, wanting to make a clean break with both their pasts. They found an apartment, and had a glorious honeymoon of sorts for three weeks. And without marking the moment as such, they passed into that space in which they were grafted onto one another, and could not henceforth part without a terrible tearing and rupture. In an informal and real sense, they were married.

And one night, as they sat on the couch, reading, she felt a strange vibration in the room. She looked up from her book and found Albert watching her, his face slightly distorted.

With dire premonition she asked, "What is it, darling?"

His voice was hard, his eyes narrowed, "I was just thinking about that dockworker you told me about," he said.

For a moment she couldn't think of what he was talking about. And then it came to her. The dockworker she had gone with shortly after her husband left her.

"I was thinking about all the things you did with him," he went on, his voice thin and febrile, "letting him fuck you in the ass, sucking his cock."

And with a slow, mounting dread she realized that his entire system was laced with scorching jealousy and anger, a pervasive and unrelenting possessiveness, spiteful and thorough. She hoped it might be a momentary mood, but at a glance she understood that she was only seeing the tip of the iceberg. For he not only remembered that one night, but had catalogued in his memory every incident she had ever told him about. He knew every action, every feeling, every moan that had been hers for the past eight years. His control was absolute.

"But that was before . . . " she began to say and stopped. What was happening was beyond logic or reason. A cold clammy hysteria clutched her belly and fear flashed in her eyes like a trapped rat in a flooded cellar. The days of physical suffering were finished, and she was returning once more to the other kind of punishment, the emotional and mental murder. Her independent self began to crumble as she found herself once again at the mercy of her vulnerability. She felt a quick impulse to flee, but was helpless against the undertow of her conditioning.

Her friend had become her husband, and he wanted revenge.

Fist Fucker

At the age of seven, Carl was taken into the old man's house, and after proper softening with ice cream, comic books, and discrete caressing, seemed to have no objection to holding the wrinkled penis in his mouth. He sucked it until it was hard, and when the sperm was plunked on his tongue, he tasted it ingeniously, not knowing that what had just happened would raise the unbridled fury of the caretakers of the world's official attitudes.

Ironically, the old man was a retired judge, and Carl's parents were pleased that their son should spend time in what they thought was an educational atmosphere. Until he was nine, Carl visited on the average of once a week, until his taste for the experience began to exceed the old man's ability to provide it. After his sombre initiation into the realm of sex, he went in search of others.

His understanding of the role of sex in society was rudimentary and inchoate. Beyond the judge's admonitions that he must never speak about what they did except to tell his parents that the nice old neighbor had read to him and given him cookies to eat, he had no grasp of the hysteria which such simple behavior as cocksucking engendered. Yet, with animal instinct, when he began his forays into the wider world, he knew to seduce only those who he sensed were willing to be had.

By the age of twelve, Carl had thrilled scores of men with his surprising eagerness to service their unspoken desires. He developed a way of standing, of looking, which set up the necessary vibrations between himself and available provender. Playing with his schoolmates, he would often disappear for an hour and prowl strange streets, finding what he wanted, and consummating his quest in hallways or cellars or the back seats of cars.

Carl knew no genital excitement himself, and was somewhat perplexed that his ministrations would bring grown men to tears. The gasps and moans which showered his ears as his delicate child's mouth would cover a cock and his tongue tingle intricate patterns over a thigh he appreciated only through empathy. What he did seemed to make others happy, and that was gratification enough.

He was first anally penetrated at the age of fourteen one summer afternoon. He was hitchhiking through the Long Island suburbs, sizing up the men who stopped for him, and either proceeding with them to a secluded space or perceiving rapidly that there was nothing to be had from that particular person. When the huge trailer stopped, the boy was taken with an unusual premonition that set him shivering. As he climbed into the cab, he was overwhelmed with an impression of muscular thighs and calloused hands. The man glanced at him once and seemed to know what Carl wanted before he even made an overture. He took the truck to a rest stop and led the boy into the back, where an entire household of furniture was stacked and being moved from South Carolina to Wyoming. It belonged to a nuclear physicist who, sickened at the corruption within the Atomic Energy Commission, had decided to become a sheep rancher.

The man pushed Carl onto a couch and stood over him, his cock straining against his pants. With expert fingers, the lad pulled the zipper down. Gently, he tugged the thickly veined tool out, and with a flutter of his eyelids, took it between his lips. He sucked for a long time, his thin young body gradually working up to a feverish pitch, tossing to and fro as he worked on the huge organ. Then, to his surprise, the man pulled back.

"Get on your stomach," the driver commanded.

Carl lay down, uncertain as to what would happen next. The man yanked his pants down, pulling them over his legs and past his feet, until the boy was naked below the waist, his slim virginal buttocks gleaming in the dull light. The man spit on his fingers and thrust them into the tiny anus, lubricating it slightly.

Without a wasted gesture, he lowered his bulk onto the child and thrust his cock into the puckered opening.

A bolt of pain shot through the boy and he gasped for breath. But hot upon the pain came a flash of sweet burning, a tender yielding that brought tears to his eyes. Grunting and huffing, the truck driver fucked the boy a long time, putting him in a dozen different positions, maneuvering the small body with ease, using his brawny arms to arrange the slender limbs in the most open poses, and then bursting in with all the power and force he could manage.

He came as the boy knelt over the arm of the couch, his buttocks raised, his legs dangling, and himself crouching behind, half raised on his toes, his heels pressed into a chest-of-drawers for leverage. As he bucked into orgasm, he drove ruthlessly into the boy's bowels and lifted him half a foot into the air.

Not long after that, Carl left home. He had already begun to see that the semi-conscious world of home and school was a restricting and artificial facade imposed over the true facts of life. He was developing a wisdom which transcended the artifacts of conventional knowledge, and he could no longer pretend to possess the naivete and immaturity expected of someone his age.

He went to San Francisco, where he discovered the baths. Because of his youth, his good looks, and his unbounded willingness to please, he soon became a favorite in gay circles. One night he was spotted by a jaded millionaire who offered to house him with the others in the harem he had built in an effort to pique a glutted appetite. Carl accepted, and within a short time ascended to the status of superstar.

But none of this seemed to affect his basic humility, and his unabashed desire to provide sexual pleasure for others. By seventeen, he was a virtuoso in the art of passive homoesexual performance, and highly skilled in all the nuances of surrender. His patron grew proud, and then jealous, of his charge, and forbid him to have contact with anyone but himself.

Soon after, he left the mansion, and on his way along a highway, accepted a ride from a bestial-looking motorcycle rider who took him to his camp, where several dozen others lounged in snarling lassitude. The boy was thrown to them the way meat is thrown to lions in a zoo, and for several days he served as a slave to their every whim, catering to their surly need for stimulation.

On the fourth day, lying over a pile of sleeping bags, having been fucked by twelve men in succession, he was initiated into the form that he had been unconsciously evolving toward for his entire life. The leader of the pack, kneeling behind him, placed his bunched fist between Carl's buttocks. The boy gasped, and then relaxed, and the huge curled hand pressed tightly against his asshole. Slowly, he gave way, and the first entered the hot opening. The universe seemed to crash about Carl's head as the man behind him continued to push, engulfing his hand, his wrist, and then his whole forearm up to the elbow. At that point, he stopped, and with a deliberate motion, flexed his entire arm, filling the pulsing channel completely with hard bulging muscle.

Carl smiled in ecstasy. After a decade of service, he felt he was finally being satisfied.

He continued drifting from adventure to adventure until one morning an eerie mood enveloped him. He was walking down a street and as he looked at the faces of the people who passed, he realized they were all asleep. He saw that, through his peculiar metamorphosis, he had become an utterly superior human being. By virtue of having lived in the realm of excess, where others were too fearful to venture, he had attained a depth of awareness that set him apart from the human herd.

Not intrinsically cerebral, and his formal education having ended early, he was not able to articulate the insight with any degree of precision. But as the bright western sun sparkled in his eyes, something like a religious revelation exploded in his brain. If it is true that a person who masters any one thing has mastered all of life itself, then he was a realized human being, for he had become an emperor of perversion.

Thereafter he wandered the country like a ghost. Men would encounter him and tell their friends of an apparition of startling beauty, who sucked cock and allowed himself to be layed and gave a pleasure that went deeper than the sexual, that ultimately soothed the soul. And if asked what he wanted in return, he would say simply, "Fist-fuck me, please," and would lie in rapture as the clenched hand went deeper and deeper into his entrails.

There is a photo of him, the only one in existence, in which he is suspended from a wooden crossbeam. He is shown being lowered onto two men, each of whom has one arm, up to the elbow, buried in his ass at the same time. The boy's eyes are closed, so it is impossible to tell what he is thinking. His face is in repose, and his body is in a state of complete relaxation. A Buddhist monk, seeing the picture, was heard to exclaim, "That is a man who has attained Nirvana."

He was found dead, at the age of twenty-four, wrapped in a mattress in a ravine outside of Los Angeles. No one knew his name or where he had come from, so he was buried in a public field. His life had been a total and selfless giving to others, and he was not known to have sought anything for himself, except the blissful trance state which occurred whenever he was lovingly fist fucked.

Several of the members of Troy Perry's Gay Church subsequently began an official movement to have him proclaimed as their first saint.

Thy Kingdom of Come

The austere freedom she discovered in masturbation razed all desire for intercourse with others. She was liberated into a strange prison, one in which she was permitted to do, or say, or feel anything she liked at any time the impulse moved her, but on one condition: that she remain alone.

That she had been gravitating toward this state during her entire adult life was something that could be seen only in retrospect. In the decade following the loss of her virginity at seventeen, she had moved through a period of such rampant promiscuity that it seemed she would never be able to get enough of people. It was impossible for her to remember how many men, women, children, animals, and dildoes had been inside her, how many gallons of sperm she had swallowed, which perverse actions she had not attempted or catered to.

Then, one night, as she lay writhing on a hooked rug before a roaring fireplace, her body a seething sea of red shadows, her fingers grappling her cunt, after hours of being fucked, whipped, pissed on, made to grovel, some delicate cord inside her snapped, and she opened her eyes to wonder why she was expending so much energy on what had suddenly come to seem a senseless melodrama. With ruthless honesty she severed truth from the appearances which camouflaged it, and asked herself the only real question which has any validity in the erotic realm: *why involve others at all?*

She went into seclusion to ponder the answer, and came to an astonishing conclusion. "Other people merely provide additional energy to increase the scope and intensity of the orgasm," she reasoned, "either by joining the fucking itself, or by watching, or by providing necessary inputs at crucial times in the form of slaps, caresses, or words." She perceived other functions, such as providing company or support or instruction, but she discounted these as pertaining to people who had not yet attained to any autonomy of personality.

"Orgasm is the quintessentially private experience," she continued, "and the notion that we must share it with others is the final corruption of what's left of civilization. The only time that people should fuck is to make babies. Everything else is sheer indulgence."

Accordingly, she locked herself in. She had her food delivered, she had her phone taken out, and she devoted herself to exploring a realm where many go with feelings of shame and defeat, but which she entered with a sense of triumph and arrival.

She prepared a single room for her ritual, sealed the window and painted every surface black, removed all the furniture except for a single mattress which she covered with a black satin sheet. Whenever she closed the door on herself, no sound or light could reach her. She was launched immediately into interior space, the turf of contemplation.

Immediately following her decision, a great peace descended upon her. The first artifact which fell away was the need to perform. It became clear at once that almost all her behavior was unconsciously geared toward some real or introjected audience, that far from being free, she had been a captive actress forced to play a multitude of roles for her parents, her lovers, her friends, her enemies, and even strangers in the street. At once her entire attitude changed, and a profound relaxation overtook her. No longer concerned with what anyone thought of her, including herself, the umbilical cord which had bound her to propriety, even when she was shrieking in wanton release running naked through a roomful of men, was cut. She saw that those actions which she had thought most uninhibited were nothing more than the strident proof of her inhibition. By herself she became truly wild, and in that wilderness found a deep calm.

And when she gave herself to masturbation, unfathomable vistas opened. Not constrained to compromise herself in order to accommodate the expectations of anyone else, she flowered in the fullness of her being. She discovered a connection between her clitoris and her third eye. As she incessantly brushed the tip of that lower instrument of pure erotic pleasure, the world of psychic reality unfolded. She could peer into past and future by seeing the present in great depth. She was able, after a while, to transcend relative time altogether and abide in the sense of the eternal. She cried out in terror once when, from a region she could not have imagined existed, she beheld the ultimate reality, the single truth which embraced all partial images. Absolute Time seized her in its jaws and laughed as she danced along the ridges of its gleaming fangs.

Her memory returned. All the scenes and feelings of childhood, so long buried, came to the surface, and for the first time in her life she was able to see her life as a single gesture, a woven fabric with a unitary design. Her body found its most meaningful expressions. As she revved up the energy in her cunt, her spine would shake, her head roll from side to side, her tongue lap the air, her legs tremble and kick, her buttocks lose their tension. Three, four, five spasms would shake her frame, but instead of having a heavy body lying on her, or an importune hand feeling her, she would be blessed with the lightness of solitude, and would rise from the floor and dance, joyously, sombrely, beautifully, all to herself, in pitch blackness, relishing that no one could see, or would ever see, the real person that she was becoming.

She destroyed all the mirrors in the apartment so she would not distract herself with her own image; she had come to view perception as an impediment to vision. She was transmogrifying into something beyond all human standards to judge, a creature of fierce tangled beauty. She lost her conventional good looks and became sublime, the way a snarled tree ravaged by wind and salt air grows terrible in its aspect on cliffs overhanging the ocean.

Occasionally, that portion of her mind which had been socially conditioned stirred itself to condemn or worry her. "You are going crazy," it said, "you have no more friends or family, you never go out, you never see people. That's unnatural, pathological." And when she withered the superego with a scorn born of solitude, it changed its attack and used the final weapon in the arsenal of those who would rob an individual of his or her personal reality.

"You have lost the ability to love," it said, "you are selfish, uncaring."

It was not too long before she saw that it was thought itself that was the real enemy, the thing that separated her from herself. During her spells in the black room, after a long long time doing nothing, letting herself be, and then gradually drifting into an awareness of her body, she would begin again the exquisite rite of masturbation. Unimpeded by the demands of another, she soared again and again into the heights of sexual ecstasy unknown by all but a few, those very few who have had the courage to admit that sex is the sister of death, and thus can only be known alone. The orgasms she experienced surpassed the paltry twitchings given to those who still require support for their pleasure, in the way that the flight of eagles goes beyond the spastic flappings of sparrows. And after returning from the mountain tops, the first thing to cast a pall upon her spirit was always language, the limitation of thought.

Her diary reads: "The space I call my *self* was clear. There was no split in me, no confusion. I was a single entity, a thing. Distinct from everything around me, yet part of it all, I had no identity at all. I don't really know how to explain it, since the experience was deeper than language. I don't know how long it lasted, for time was not relevant.

"Then something stirred. I sensed it the way one might be aware of the movement of a small animal in tall grass. I felt as though some precious balance were being lost, some vital equilibrium. And in the wake of that feeling, the words appeared.

"They flew across my mind like the banners tied to dirigibles which sweep across the skies on summer afternoons. I watched, and for a few seconds they were just another phenomenon, no different than the beating of my heart, the coursing of my blood, the rhythms of my breath. The words had no special weight. They were merely aspects of the all.

"But some strange and hideous transformation began to take place, and they started to grow stronger, louder. It was as though they weren't content to be part of my being, they demanded dominance of it. I became annoyed and turned my attention to see what they wanted. And in that instant of shifting center, I realized that T had returned. There was suddenly a platform of observation which was removed from the process being observed.

"Like a person caught in the net of a suffocating nightmare, I struggled. But as I fought, the words proliferated. They poured into my consciousness from a thousand sources, booming, crackling, sighing, shouting. Strings of sentences intertwined and formed fantastic patterns which came to constitute the stuff of images.

"And from that whirling energy concentration of exploding verbiage, pictures were born, faces of real and imagined creatures, denizens of memory and desire who proceeded to act out intricate dramas in which I was invariably a hero or a victim. I was swept into a maelstrom of abstraction, and was drawn, gasping, into the symbolic world, the fantasmagoric kingdom of concepts.

"I was *thinking* again."

As she approached a state of brute intelligence, a stark sensitivity to the fact of existence, rationalization fell from her like dead skin from a shedding snake. She emerged cleansed of all the impacted overlay of culture which had been grafted onto her soul from the very first moment she became a seed growing in her mother's belly.

On the day of her thirtieth birthday, she had achieved an unquenchable autonomy. As she took herself to her room to masturbate, she was so filled with herself that it seemed no external force could ever impinge upon her again. But as she reached down to cover her cunt with her hand, the space around her was slowly suffused with a golden light.

She stared in dumb wonder at the phenomenon. In front of the mattress, a curtain of silver needles shimmered and took shape, until a tall naked man, with green skin and long curly violet hair appeared, his red eyes piercing her gaze, his succulent cock throbbing gently. Her surprise was total, and she did not stir, but continued to lie there, her legs parted, her breasts lolling on her chest, her mouth wet and open, her fingers spreading the cleft between her thighs.

"Very nice," he said.

She blinked. "Who are you?" she asked, the first words she had spoken to anyone in almost three years.

He smiled. "I have been called many names, not all of them complimentary. I have been known as Zeus, as Jehovah, as Baal, as Thor. I am who am, and all that, and have assumed a thousand forms. But most people nowadays refer to me as GOD."

"God?" she whispered. "But I thought there was no God."

"Many people have denied my existence," he said with a droll intonation, "even to my face. It's part of the overall perversity of human beings."

"But what are you doing here?" she asked.

"You have attracted me," he told her. "As your species falls further and further into conformity and mediocrity, I find fewer and fewer occasions to visit earth. In fact, I come so infrequently that there is a rumor that I have died. I used to stay here a lot, in the old days, when there were some fantastic people on the globe. And you're the first thing to arrive in a long time that's got that kind of quality."

"But of what conceivable interest could I be to you?" she said. After having learned to discard the company of people as something trivial, she was amazed that God would seek that very thing.

"Why, to fuck you, of course," God replied, and laughed, a deep baritone rumble. "Why else?"

She raised herself on one elbow. "To fuck what you have created? That doesn't make sense."

"Oh, I haven't created anything," God said, sinking to the floor and sitting on the edge of the mattress. "I'm just here, like the rest of you. The only difference is that you come and go, and I'm immortal." He scratched his head. "It's really very peculiar. I mean, I just woke up one day and found that I was God. I couldn't remember what happened before I was born, didn't know where I came from, and knew that I would always be. I've seen universes come and go, worlds born and die. I am old beyond any comprehension you might have, and yet I am always fresh, always new. I am the synthesis of all contradictions. I. . ."

He smiled again, and broke off "But you've heard me

described well enough by your own prophets and poets. No need to give you a resume."

She sat up. "But if all this is true, why should you want something as limited as fucking?"

He reached forward and stroked one of her breasts. "Well, for me, everything is limited. To amuse myself I have to make my choice among limitations. And on the scale I see things from, one limitation is no different from any other. For example, I just came from watching an entire galaxy explode, a happening that had been building for seventy-nine quadrillion years. It covered a space your mind couldn't begin to encompass. And that was interesting. But then I wondered what to do next and I thought, 'I haven't been to earth for a while, let me go see if there's anybody around worth fucking these days.' I scanned the planet and was discouraged at first glance. I saw nothing but a plethora of such shallow sensualists that it made my cock-form shrivel. Why, the very sexes themselves are on the verge of total alienation from one another. But on a second look around, I saw you. And here I am. Although, in a sense, since I am everywhere, I have been here all along."

"And you want *me*?" she asked, beginning to be impressed with the enormity of the personage who stood before her. She put one hand on her hair and said, "I must look a mess."

He laughed again. "Your lapse into vanity is charming, my dear," he said, "but I wouldn't have come if you weren't beyond judging things by the standards of the crowd. I'm not interested in anyone until he or she has gone beyond the illusion of group standards and has hacked a hard-won path through all the tedious variations on the public sexual act, including that which requires fantasy for its completion. I want a soul that has striven to burst the bonds of common understanding and can appreciate the unique."

He lowered his head and stared between her thighs. "When you fuck me, you can experience everything you have when you are alone—everything. And I will infuse that state with such awesome power that you could never even dream of with your puny human faculties. With your mind, you can grasp the structure of the universe; with mine, you can see into the heart of the void from which all existence springs."

"And what do you get out of it?" she asked.

"Just a piece of ass," God said. "My tastes are simple."

She pulled her knees to her chest and wrapped her arms around her shins. "I'm not sure I want to," she told him, "even if you are God. I've worked hard to get where I am. Why should I give you pussy? I'm happy with the dimensions I already know."

He pursed his lips. "I can make it worth your while," he answered.

"Well, how good a fuck can you be? You're still in the form of a man. That thing between your legs is only a cock."

"I don't claim any special skill," he replied. "But I can offer you something else."

"You mean you want to *pay* me?" she asked.

"I can offer you Heaven," he said.

"Heaven!" she exclaimed. "You mean there's really a Heaven too?"

"Oh, nothing like they tell you about in Sunday school. It's a bit more chic than that. More like a private club, for my special friends." She regarded him suspiciously and shifted her weight. "You really do have a nice ass," he said. And then, with an abrupt change of tone, continued, "Whichever God made me God seems to have defined my powers clearly. I can't create anything new, but I can change the nature of what already exists; I can do things with what's already here."

He waited a long time in silence, and then in a hushed whisper said, "I can make you *immortal*."

Her jaw fell open. "Immortal?" she repeated. "You mean . . . to live . . . forever?"

"That's right," he said, his expression smug. He hunched over, and his words came out quickly. "The fact of the matter is, earth is the only place in all of creation that has fucking. And so, while it isn't the most spectacular activity available, its rarity gives it a certain value. I've granted the boon of eternal life to several thousand others in the course of your history, and if you accept my offer, I will remove you to a planet that you will share with them. Once there, you can have the company of the greatest fuckers that the world has ever seen, or all the privacy you desire. And when I'm in the area, every few million years or so, I'll drop by."

"So I become your mistress."

"Call it what you like," he said. He looked into her eyes, holding her gaze, and went on in a chill voice. "The alternative, if you refuse, is to live out your days and end, like everyone else, in the grave." The last word sent shivers down her spine, and he finished, "What have you got to lose by saying yes, and what can you possibly gain by saying no?"

She waited a long moment and answered, "My integrity. A whore's a whore even if she's God's whore." And then let the breath out of her lungs with a loud sigh and added, "This is just like the scene with the tree in the garden. Where's Satan?"

"God laughed. "Don't you know? I'm Satan too. I just haven't bothered to split roles this time."

"Is this the only game you know?" she said, slightly disgusted.

"For humanity, it's the only game in town," he said. "If you are true to yourself, you will refuse the fuck, and die forever. But if you sell out, you get paradise as a reward."

She lay back down again, her whole being filled with the prospect of realizing the one dream that has haunted the species since it first became aware of death, the hope of immortality. She balanced it against every earthly value she had come to cherish. His hands stroked her calves as she wrestled with the problem. And without being fully aware of what was happening, she sank into a lassitude that was the prelude to capitulation.

Her mind swam lazily in its thoughts. The single word "forever" sounded in her psyche like a gong. And finally, she succumbed. The temptation was too strong, the offer too compelling.

"All right," she said, "you win."

Her thighs parted and her stomach swelled with a deep breath. "You can fuck me," she told him.

God moved forward until he was between her legs, her wet cunt staring up at him, her hips beginning to rotate. But as he approached, she put her hands on his shoulders and held him for a second. She looked him in the eyes.

"Just don't get me pregnant," she said. And then took God's huge hard cock into her, opening the doors to eternal life.

A COLLECTION OF BONES

essays on the erotic experience

Once upon a time, in ancient India, a woman ran away from her husband's house, and went along a road leading to the village where her parents lived. She saw an old man, a sage, sitting by the path, and, feeling reckless, smiled at him seductively. The man glanced up, and upon seeing her flashing teeth, realized that a skeleton stood before him, its flesh no more significant than the clothes the body wore.

A half hour later, the husband passed by the same spot. He stopped before the sage and asked, "Did you see a woman go by this way?"

The sage replied, "Whether what went along here was a man or a woman, I do not know. But a collection of bones is moving down this road."

Buddhist Tales

The true metaphysicians are found among the debauchees, not elsewhere.

E. M. Cioran

Author's Note

Since writing The Metasexual Manifesto, I have attempted, in my own life, to extirpate the entrenched linguistic prejudices rooted in the failure to make the necessary distinction between sex and metasex. This has proven extremely difficult, and my sympathies extend to those who, upon reading the essay, try to program a new semantic into their word-thought forms.

For a while, I toyed with the idea of going through all my previous works and substituting the word "metasex" where I had inaccurately used "sex." But this would have been a falsification of record, obscuring the outlines of the development of my erotic evolution, as well as a stylistic awkwardness, so I have let the original usage remain.

The essays may seem to contradict one another, but this is due to my having lived each erotic aspect through to its conclusion and articulating that conclusion in rather absolutist terms. Also, the works show the struggle to formulate an idea more than the polished presentation of an established concept. I hope the value of the thought renders the crudity of expression irrelevant.

The erotic descriptions in the essays contain no exaggeration. The notion of a state which transcends erotic duality is based on experience, not speculation.

Bodhi Is the Body

Perhaps the most common trap surrounding the notion of enlightenment is viewing it as a state divorced from the moment-to-moment experience of life, as though it were some kind of paradisical attainment which transcends earthly existence. People attempt to "reach it" in the same way they might run after a bus.

Enlightenment can be simply defined as an a-historical state of awareness shaped by the historical matrix within which it arises, having no meaning apart from the genetic structure of the individual who lives in that state. Thus, the understanding of a person of three thousand years ago is at once the same as and different from that of someone alive today.

One thing has, however, remained fairly constant throughout the ages, and that is the fact that enlightenment has been almost exclusively a man's game. Women have been considered at best irrelevant and at worst ruinous, in the quest for truth. In less hypocritical times, this was stated openly by the priests of all the major religions; today the notion has gone underground, but is more pernicious for just that reason.

The insight into this issue came to me, as many of my most acute visions do, while I was fucking. To describe what she and I did, the feelings which flowed, the passions that informed our behavior, would not be to the point. What takes place between a man and woman when they return to the Source is far deeper than language. We fucked and we made love; we did both, shifting from an activity in which two individuals act upon one another, to a movement of a single entity that no longer distinguished among its parts. The night was a reality with the quality of a dream, and hummed with that singular vibration of union, where subjective and objective interpenetrate like the blue and red of yin and yang.

The violet ecstasy of those hours entered me with all the significance of a childhood imprinting. As I lay in her arms, her body an undulating density of corduroy coils, the smells and sounds and textures of our dance conjured a realm of awareness in which the chains of time were shattered.

And with apparent incongruity, a line from an old book came into my consciousness: "When one is ready, the teacher will appear."

I was at a stage where I had been doing a particular kind of work, using Gurdjieffian methods of self observation, paying attention to the physical aspects of my being . . . posture, gesture, facial expressions, the sound of my voice, movements. Without any effort at changing myself in a given direction, I adhered simply to the discipline, and the work had begun to show a result. I was beinning to find many facets of my existence clarified, and doorways to so-called higher states were opening. Questions which had tortured me were seen through, and debilitating habits fell away. No decisions were involved; the process of self-observation made all things obvious. As I became aware of myself, the workings of the universe made themselves known.

Concurrently, I wondered from time to time whether some "master" would pop up one day to take me by the hand and lead me to realms of knowledge closed to ordinary mortals. But it was not until I spent that night with Julia that the basic prejudice which lies at the root of so many schools of enlightenment flashed in all its dimensions. Something about the concept of esoteric wisdom had long bothered me, and now I could see what it was: in its continual pointing to a condition removed from day-to-day life, most of the supposedly spiritual literature had dropped women to the status of hindrance. Without its being stated in so many words, it was assumed that no woman could ever be a teacher, or if one were, then would have to operate in the capacity of a man's role.

As we took to one another's arms and legs and eyes, and I was infused with a stinging alertness, I saw that she was giving me, at that very moment, lessons about the meaning of life that were as profound as anything any teacher or master had ever talked about. From terror to bliss, all the modes of being triumphed between us. She was providing me with the completion without which all verbal knowledge is fatuous mumbling. While I had vaguely been expecting a bearded and robed Indian expatriate, the truths I was so hungrily seeking were pressed tightly against me, in the shape of a mouth against my mouth, and a vortex of energy which called me into the hot wet center of her body. Singing and sweating the wondrous song of sex, we were joined in full intimate contact with the living embodiment of our primary reality as human beings.

"All this," I thought, "through contact with a woman. All this, through the vehicle of sex."

In a very important sense, my life had been a struggle to come to terms with women, beginning, of course, with my mother. In doing that I was, without articulating it as such, defining what it meant to be a man. I had spent many years in the boundless stretches of homosexuality, and despite the treasures I had found there, saw that that style of life, if followed exclusively, was, for me, ultimately sterile. It did not, by itself, replenish the juices I needed to sustain me.

With women, I had practiced a judicious promiscuity, and even when I lived with a woman for any length of time, I could not appreciate her as anything but a minor incident in my life. I was infected with the thought that someday I would meet a teacher, a man, who would show me the way. It took many years of work and the help of a woman therapist to point out that *the man I was looking for was myself.*

Like so many of my generation, I ransacked the wardrobe of Eastern thought for answers, and found the same spectrum available as in the West, couched in different terminology. It went from folksy wisdom to obscure mystifications and occasionally, as in Ch'an Buddhism, a perfectly penetrating truth. But for all the value of these aphorisms and instructions, none of those hundreds of thousands of words helped fill the very real hole in my psyche. The greatest help I received from the East was the assurance that I wasn't the only one facing the thorny problems of living by attempting to contact the vibration of universal consciousness. The greatest damage done by my foray into Oriental attitudes was the perpetuation of the notion that enlightenment is a state which precludes, or ignores, continuing relationship with women.

The following story exemplifies this attitude in perhaps its mildest form. A Zen master and his disciple were walking along and came to a stream where a woman stood by the shore, not wanting to wet her robes in crossing. The master picked her up and carried her across. He and the student continued for several miles and the disciple finally burst out, "It is against all our teaching to have anything to do with women, and yet you picked her up in your arms." The master snorted, "I put her down at the far end of the stream, but you, it seems, have been carrying her in your mind all this way."

The story is used to point up the process whereby we are trapped by conceptual thought, and as such is a salutary tale. One is very prone to admire the old monk for his greater "humanity." But several questions are raised, such as, "What sort of teaching is it that treats women as a species of psychic lepers, to be avoided at all costs?" And, "What sort of society is it in which a woman comes to view herself as so inept and frail she can't cross a stream by herself?"

One here gets into the trickier question as to whether there is something in the nature of woman that is intrinsically disruptive to a man's peace of mind. God knows, any man who has become involved with a woman has certainly been tempted to quit their company forever and choose monastic seclusion as a viable alternative. But if peace of mind has to be bought at the price of the exclusion of half the species from meaningful social intercourse, then one must call into doubt any so-called higher state of consciousness available only under that condition.

Putting aside the contention of the sexual nihilists that men and women are inherently damaging to one another's well-being, the cause for such a split between male and female is to be sought in conditioned attitudes toward the problem. There are certainly times when a man must be alone, and times when he must be in the exclusive company of other men. But to raise such a cyclical psychological process to the level of a permanent and laudable condition, and then to bolster it with ideological argument, is pathological.

In the West, beginning with the Pauline misogyny, women have been held by official Christian spokesmen to be little better than slaves, and the sex with which they tempt men has been considered the most cunning work of the devil. To counterbalance this, the Church raised Mary to the status of supervirgin, making her equally unreal. Popes have blessed armies with holy water, sending them happily off to slaughter, and then promulgated laws which condemn teenagers for necking. I don't know why I expected anything better from the East. Stupidity is not the special province of any hemisphere or nation or creed. As in any given sampling of any portion of humanity, in this area there are a few who have attained wholeness, and the rest stumble along in different stages of waking sleep, using more or less satisfying rationalizations to hide their basic fear.

Enlightened men may choose, for their own reasons, to remove themselves from the company of women. In our time, Thomas Merton comes to mind. Others, equally fulfilled creatures, may not. Alan Watts is an example. It is when the private solution of a strong man is turned into a rule for others to live by that the damage is done. I knew a woman who was capable of total orgasmic release. She had no problem with the quibble as to whether orgasms are clitoral or vaginal. When she came, she came entirely, from her toes to her brain, shivering, bursting, melting, burning, climaxing fully. She began to study with a hatha yoga teacher, a sweet old man who had founded an institute and culled a following from several thousand of the disenfranchised young of America.

His mastery of the asanas was unquestioned, and his desire to help humanity was sincere. Yet, he managed to insinuate such an atmosphere of ethereal pseudo-spirituality that his students saw giving up sex as a mark of progress toward some mystical goal. The woman, her eyes possibly blinded by the thick haze of incense which hung over the institute, lost sight of the fact that yoga is primarily a process for keeping the body strong, the mind clear, the heart capable of loving. She rejected sex, and commenced to spend much of her time in a trance-like state which she identified with cosmic calm. Half a year later, she was utterly dispirited, and despite the regularity of her new-found habits, she had let slip the *elan vital*, that spark of vivacity which is the sign of the sexually alert person. With the revivifying power of the orgasm denied her, her body no longer thrilled with energy. She lost her zest for living and became an automaton.

This is not to denounce yoga, but the imposition of a poorly understood worldview on a set of exercises. Nor is there anything necessarily wrong with celibacy. There are circumstances in which celibacy is the natural order of things. A person who loses a mate, for example, may not be able to fuck for a long period of time. This is simple bio-psychology. Or a person may be jaded through sexual overstimulation, and will need some time to lie fallow. Or a person may come to a point at which sex ceases to operate through the genital channels. And, of course, there is with age and/or wisdom, a gradual refinement of the uses of sexual energy altogether.

These are all organic processes. But to make an a priori value of celibacy, however, and to claim that to stop fucking will bring one closer to God or enlightenment, is, categorically, a pathological defense on the part of a person who is sick in his or her sex, and is reaching for the most grandiose rationalization by which to defend that perversion.

I returned to my own experience to find what was true for me. This much I knew: to fuck a woman that I care for and to melt into orgasm with her, subsumes all that is fine in life. In fact, I found that unless all the rest of my life was in order, I was not free to partake of that sublime experience. The orgasm is *the* life-enhancing process. From its physiological function of discharging tension and toning the organism, to its biological function of improving the quality of children that are born, to its spiritual function of putting one in touch with higher forms of energy, it contains all the keys anyone might want. Sex is a complete activity, bringing all the fragments into a whole, operating as the most subtle and immediate communication between human being and human being. It acts resoundingly to affirm the pulse of life; in its contractions and expansions, it is the pulse of life itself. How on earth, I wondered, could anyone view it as anything but a central factor in a person's attempts to live most fully?

It did not take too long to see that such an attitude arises through the failure of teachers and so-called holy men to come to terms with their feelings about women. Seemingly, they have not been able to deal with their fear, their confusion, their loathing, their need, their desire, their hidden worship, of women. With a shift that has become the mark of our history, they separated the genders in their own context, and made enlightenment a preserve for men only, in the same way that the Catholic Church has decreed that no woman is good enough to hold the consecrated host in her fingers. Those women who did try to crash the gates became grotesques, like St. Theresa, with her scorching visions of angels piercing her bowels with flaming spears, and Madam Blavatsky, who could out-think, out-curse, and out-maneuver any man who came into her vicinity, and won her theosophical spurs over the heads of men who were thrillingly eager to feel her psychic lash across their metaphysical buttocks. But such women only underscore the hidden thrust of the sacred teachings, the one sentence that probably has never been spoken, but lies at the core of all major religious systems: that one can not learn anything from a woman that is of any real value on the road to enlightenment, and that any sexual contact with women is at best a distraction from the process of seeking truth.

Although he never addressed himself to the problem directly, it was Wilhelm Reich who most forcefully, among men, cut through the obfuscation. To ring in such a complex and heroically tragic man with just a few words is perhaps unfair, and I can only pay my way toward doing that by urging the reading of his work. It was his observation that when the life energy which flows through us is blocked, distorted, or "armored" as a result of growing up in a particular civilization, total orgasmic release is impossible. So far as I know, he is the only one to differentiate between mere ejaculation for the male, or clitoral/vaginal stimulation for the female, and the full vegetative rush of complete orgasm. In a condition of orgastic impotence, the person will manifest one of two basic characterological states:

fascism or mysticism. Either there will be a softening of the self-sense, in which the person loses all awareness of boundary; or there is a hardening, in which rigid boundaries become the central aspect of the life style. One need not be too sophisticated to see that these are indeed the ruling modes of social life in the world today. The governments and official institutions are almost totally fascistic in their machine-like quest to impose conformist order on all human beings, while the masses of people stagger around in an obscurantism relieved only by their vague mystical yearnings, their hope for salvation from above.

To extrapolate from that vision to the topic at hand, it is necessary only to point out that what has been denied to women is the acknowledgement that they are teachers of life in their very bodies. Very few women I have known have possessed this awareness of their own biological efficacy. The sickness of mankind has been the overwhelming importance placed on discursive thinking, to the detriment of the life processes at large. Women, who instinctively understand the severe limitations of conceptual thought, have not only been relegated to second place, but have been forced to deny their immediate perception of the true hierarchy of value. When a woman says in scorn and sorrow, "You only want me for my body, don't you?," neither she nor the man she addresses usually has any inkling of the profundity of the insight contained in the question.

For what the man wants is to *feel his own body*, and it is with practically automatic tropism that he reaches to a woman, to sense his palpable reality by embracing a person who is fully alive inside herself. Those women who have attained this awareness form the heart of the current phase of women's perpetual struggle for liberation. But these very women then refuse to serve as psychophysical wet nurses, to be available to men who are still allowing themselves to be transmogrified into robots.

What men need right now, more than anything, is the ability to be in touch with their own feelings. And the only men who, as a self-identified group, are freeing themselves to feel, are gays. There is a strong argument to be made for the notion that homosexuality should be the general sexual form of the future, with heterosexual unions forming a minority, but even if that were so, historical intransigence is unlikely to allow it. The majority, the heterosexuals who run the machines of civilization, will most likely grow more and more alienated from their animal sensibility, men becoming plastic automatons and women continuing to trudge behind, and produce either a world of grey uniformity or the next and utterly cataclysmic war.

To know oneself as a body is more important, at this moment in history, than to read the words of all the wise men who have ever lived. The enlightenment game, as it is classically played, has degenerated to a pathetic masturbation, fit only for men who are still seeking their lost fathers and afraid to accept the sexuality of their mothers. It is ironic that yoga has become such a fad, for the sense of the word is "to join," giving the idea of union. But the union most naturally available to us, the coupling in the sexual act, is losing its healing function. To deny this embrace, or to turn it into a sensual pastime, or to base it on ideas of conquest, is to kill any real chance of understanding what life is all about. For if in our time, a man and a woman cannot experience sex except as a symbol, then total insanity is upon us.

The truth of the matter is this: when one picks up a handful of earth, that dirt is the stuff of existence. Existence is not an idea. It is the air we breathe, the food we eat, the sun that warms us. Only the diseased imaginations of those who are incapable of orgasmic release produce fantasies of a reality other than that which explodes and murmurs within us and without us from moment to moment, on all its planes and levels, endlessly. Reality is known through the trembling awareness of the immediate now, a now which includes all that has been and all that will be. All allusions to things which are somehow "other," other dimensions, others beings, gods and goddesses, refer to manifestations which, if they have any existence, do not have existence independent of our own. To seek salvation by fleeing to another psychic state is like attempting to escape the ocean by switching from one raft to another. Anything which exists exists within the matrix of total creation. The stupefying wonder of the universe is not what it is, but THAT IT IS. The things which present themselves to our senses, including the mind sense, can be beautiful or ugly, intricate or simple, tremendous or trivial. And to the degree that we are scientists, we can spend our time in figuring how the different configurations of our energy relate. But to get so involved trying to negotiate some phantasmagoric psychic labyrinth to the detriment of the sense of wonder and awe, and to the point of distracting us from real questions, such as, "Does everyone have enough to eat?" is to miss the universe for the ego. How insane to be so busy searching for enlightenment that one can't see the glow of love in the eyes of a person just a few feet away.

The distinction between Existence and Being is clear. And insofar as our bodies are impermanent, we ought to not be attached to them, mistaking this momentary manifestation for total reality. Yet, there is no reality apart from the body. The body is the way in which one aspect of Being knows itself through Existence. To know the body is to know all that one can ever know, and to know what one cannot know.

Any process of enlightenment which degrades the fact of the body by rejecting sex is perverse. Any teacher who does not realize and admit the nature of women, as bodies, into his teaching, is a neurotic charlatan. If Adam and Eve do not find a way to get it together, the species will not survive.

The notion that women and sex have been excluded from the area of seeking truth might seem an overstatement, but consider the common prejudice which keeps most of us from wondering whether Buddha continued fucking after his satori. The legend has it that after he became enlightened, his wife became a nun. And what of Jesus? What mammoth insensitivity is involved in presuming that he had nothing to learn in the arms of Mary Magdalen? Did Meher Baba fuck? Does Krishnamurti fuck? These questions seem blasphemous. Yet why should that be if we were not so conditioned to believe that holiness and wisdom are incompatible with sexuality, that an enlightened man will no longer have intimate contact with a woman's body?

In the act of fucking, a woman can teach a man lessons of life he cannot find in any book or the rigamarole of any sect. If only he knows how to read them. If only she is aware of them herself. A man who cannot learn from a woman, a naked woman vibrantly alive with pure passion of living, is no longer human, no matter how elevated his station or glorious his rhetoric.

On that night with Julia, I felt that realization with a sense of homecoming. There, in the cock and cunt, in the heat and patterns, in the movement and stillness, in the sound and silence, in the pervasively private moments when male and female join to become a single entity, is the key to our search for meaning.

The Trucks

Eleven o'clock on a Friday night in early October on Greenwich Street. The warehouse district. The sidewalks are deserted, the air is close, polluted. Nearby, the Hudson River flows in turgid currents, sweeping its daily quotient of garbage and industrial waste into New York Bay.

I walk along quickly, my eyes darting ahead, ready to leap into the street at the first hint of attack and run for my life. Survival in the city parallels survival in the jungle: the existence of natural enemies is real. The chance that someone wanting to take my money or my life lurks in a hallway or behind a car is not so low that I can afford to be careless.

I am angry that I can't take a peaceful stroll at night without having my lungs filled with poison and my vibrations challenged by the threat of violence. I spit on the civilization which bore me: two thousand years of greed, bigotry, ugliness, alienation from the ground-of-being, and it ends by fouling its own nest, turning the verdant earth into a ghastly horror show.

Up ahead I see a group of five men lounging against a car. My heart begins to beat and the reflex adrenalin rushes start. It is amazing that I am so conditioned to violence that it is the first thing I expect in such circumstances. I realize that an overt attack might even be welcome after the daily round of deadened hostility which living in poverty and over-crowding engenders, the day-to-day situation of all but a precious few in the "empire city."

My realistic calculation is that little more than a barrage of hard glances will be hurled at me as I pass. More psychic damage. But as I approach, and they look at me, one of them smiles. I hesitate, slow down, and look into his eyes. His gaze is soft, relaxed. There isn't murder in his heart, but an invitation to tenderness.

At once I realize the truth. They are homosexuals. I am safe!

At that moment, the radical aspect of the gay life style flashed fully in my consciousness for the first time. For all the damage they share with the rest of society, manifesting as various forms of fear, confusion, and over-reaction, I had never witnessed an instance of unprovoked physical aggression on the part of any homosexual I have ever known or observed in my entire life. I remembered that when I was young, a boy who wouldn't fight was called a sissy, and that same perversion of values, whereby the violent are honored and the peaceful are mocked, was continuing through all strata of supposedly adult society.

I moved into the circle of men the way a dog might, tentatively approaching, sniffing, psychically touching noses, proceeding to genitals and assholes. If a dog finds other dogs and a sense of community is established, the pack romps together. If there isn't, they part without a backward glance. As monkeys, we are not far removed from such a straightforward biological program, except that our civilization has robbed us of the chance to perceive one another in such direct ways.

Here, it was different. One of the men asked me for the time. I asked for a cigarette. A few pleasantries were exchanged. We all looked quite openly at one another's bodies. And suddenly, I was absorbed. With hardly a word exchanged, with no rationalizations, I simply became part of the circle, and then there were six men standing idly on the sidewalk.

Although I didn't articulate it as such at the time, the group was an energy vortex. The men were doing nothing but *being-there*. And in a period of time, their vibrations blended and formed a lazy current into which anyone passing might easily be pulled, to add his own energy to the scene. We were simply enjoying the fact of our existence and giving one another the recognition of presence. There was no need to exchange names, personal histories, opinions. The gestalt found its own pulse, and that was the pertinent reality. For there was nowhere to go, nothing to do, and we didn't have to have a reason for living.

We were alive on the earth, digging the fabulous quality of the mundane, sharing intimations of eternity.

Behind us, some ten yards away, four trucks were parked in a huge empty lot, surrounded on two sides by high brick walls and on the third by ribbed metal doors which, during the day, opened into a storehouse. It was very dark and I couldn't make out any detail. But every once in a while a man would emerge from behind a truck and walk off, or someone would come strolling down the street and drift in, almost as though to fill the slot just left empty. Obviously, something was happening and I disengaged from the circle, as easily as I had entered it, and went to see.

There were some fifty men in the concrete corral, an area some forty by fifteen feet. The scene resembled nothing so much as a small herd of steer breathing in place. There was no sense of movement anywhere; everyone was just standing. Again, I marvelled that I felt no apprehension at walking into a dark spot on a dangerous street amidst a group of strange men.

The nucleus was in one corner and most of the men formed several loose concentric circles around some activity which I couldn't see. Inside the clump of bodies at the core there was some stirring. Men drifted out toward the periphery and back in toward the center in random patterns. Four or five men were at the opposite end of the lot, waiting for something to develop in their vicinity.

I worked my way through the wall of bodies until I came to the focus of all the energy. A short thin wiry man of about twenty-five, with curly black hair and bushy sideburns, was kneeling in front of a blond giant with a body like an Olympic swimmer and a face like a Hitler Youth. The young god looked unblinkingly into the distance, his face a mask of stern composure, as the man before him worked feverishly, sucking his erect cock in and out of his mouth.

Sex itself is not sexy. Once one is actually into the contact of skin and skin, once that secret pact of silent penetration has taken place, and two human beings are totally engaged in the powerful simplicity of the act, then all thoughts of sex disappear before the thing itself. That is the state of sex, and it is an intensely private place, even when it appears in public. I wondered at the spectacle. To explain it in terms of exhibitionism and voyeurism would be to oversimplify the phenomenon to the point of destroying the astounding wealth of harmonics and overtones being produced. The ambience at that instant was such that I had difficulty catching my breath. Something stronger than cocksucking was going on there. Important and entrenched taboos were being violated. Laws were being broken. The thing that society stridently abhors was being perpetrated, and the ensuing vibration was volatile.

There was no jostling, no anxiety. The men stood quite calmly. Yet each was cunningly focussed on the balance of the mood. They were watching the cocksucker, but there was no prurient interest. Rather, the sense was that of a kind of liberation, a throwing off of shackles. The fact that this was going on in the street overwhelmed all other considerations, and pointed up the factors which keep us all from spontaneous expression of sexual affection: our own conditioned inhibitions, social censure, and legal stricture.

In this light, what was happening behind the trucks was precisely a neat bit of leaderless behavioral engineering. Anyone with any sexual sophistication understands that the crucial variables in sex, as in tripping, are set and setting. If one puts oneself in a situation in which desire can flourish into overt intercourse, then, given the proper vibration between the parties involved, if one is blessed by an erotic stirring and finds in reciprocated, it should be possible to get right into it.

Here, fifty men gathered together for no other reason than to see whether any or all of them would, in one way or another, share a moment of sexual surrender. And they were braving the demons of repression by being open enough to suck cock in public. The mood of that meeting was as exalted as any I have ever been to. Although I was probably the only one there interested in the politics of the thing. I repeat, there was as much real revolution taking place in that open crypt as in any other activity going on anywhere among the forces of life on this earth. What happened there transcended the notion of homosexuality.

The man next to me was six feet tall, black, round, and horny.

It was both easy and excruciatingly difficult to do what I wanted to do just then. For all my metaphysical meandering, the idea of sinking to my knees and acknowledging my desire so openly made me hesitate. I tested my responses, and concluded that if I were alone with the man, I would not hesitate to suck the cock which was already bulging in his jeans. I felt the familiar pressure in my chest, the slight tug at the corners of my mouth. I have blown many men, in beds, in hallways, in the baths. There is nothing more I need know about the act itself, or about my motivations in performing it. It is nothing more than a taste I own, as I do for hot buttered croissants at Sutter's. It is likely that I have known all the variations to the act. Then why there? Why then?

I think as much to prove the point to myself as it was for any purpose of sensual gratification. I would not have been at peace with myself had I not done the thing which I felt I must do in order to plumb the circumstance to its depths. And as a hundred eyes watched, I began the timeless ritual of falling slowly and consciously to my knees, letting my jaw drop open, letting my lips be full and my tongue be easy, and awaiting the pleasure of the man who stood over me.

As I entered the dance whose details have been known and described countless times by gay writers through the centuries, I entered a space of reverie. The cocksucking was not relegated to the mechanical, but to the peripheral. After all, I had a relatively large and attentive audience; I had no worry that I would not be appreciated. It was clear that at that moment. I was the focus of energy, and I didn't need to strain. The man attached to the cock in my mouth was presumed to be in command of his own decisions. If what I did ceased to interest him, he could pull out without bad feelings on anyone's part.

It was this very dissociation which gave rise to an interesting insight, which is that excitement is generally an affectation. It is the product of the sexual energy crashing against more or less aesthetic, but always negative, internal and external resistances. The ideal sexual act has no friction, and therefore no heat. It is the form taken by pure vibrant energy within and between the b dies. And so it was with perfect *sang froid* that I charted the course of his orgasm through the tactile faculties of my lips, tongue, and mouth. When he came, my only feeling was delight, and his sperm was delicious.

My only complete homosexual experience as a teenager had been with Ralph. We had gone to Randall's Island to play "chance apiece," a game in which each of us got to dry-hump the other for sixty seconds. Ralph had caught my eye during a circle-jerk among the younger boys he oversaw; we were thirteen and he was sixteen and presided over our antics with feigned boredom, pretending to attend merely out of anthropological necessity. But when he asked me to bicycle to the island with him, I knew he had chosen me as "his" and was blushingly flattered.

Of course, the code of the neighborhood insisted that I maintain a pose of gruffness, or else be thought, "queer." Odd that the honest enjoyment of a perfectly beautiful interchange between men should be branded as sinful by society at large and a model of hypocrisy planted in its place. Yet such is the culture that we live in. Of all of us, only Joey was brave, and when his mother was at her job, he would invite the gang to stand around the bed and masturbate over him as he fingered himself and brought himself to a frantic climax with a thick broomstick. The simple urge to couple, forbidden by his culture, forced him into such grotesqueries. I often wonder what became of him (I wouldn't recognize him now if I saw him) and pay him belated homage.

Ralph and I pretended to wrestle until it became quite obvious to both of us that we were interested in his fucking me, and were ready to cast off the formalities of the neighborhood code which required equal time from both partners in both directions. He lay on his back and I squatted over him, wondering whether anyone was watching and could see that we were not really wrestling, until he pushed me off him, pulled his cock out, and spilled the semen on the grass. Then—and this picture is indelibly inscribed in my memory—he wiped the tip of his cock against a tree, an action I found, and still find, absolutely startling.

We did not speak or exchange glances and rode with muted excitement back to the neighborhood and went down to the cellar where we had our clubhouse. The vibrations were thick.

Up to that moment, even our indiscretions had been within ethical bounds, but what was being suggested by our mood took us into very dangerous territory. For a trembling teenager born and raised in an Italian neo-feudalism, the ramifications of my desire were immense. What we were about to do was *worse than sin*, it was *disgusting*.

Yet, the thin troubled teenager that I was could find no reason in my body or heart or mind to deny what so strongly called to me. This was the problem of sexual freedom in its sharpest outline. Both of us were too unlettered even to know the word homosexual. Our knowledge of sex was rudimentary, and in a sense, quite healthy. Pole went into hole, that was all we knew. And now, after decades of sexual libertinism, I find that after all there is little more to it than that. The richness lies in the depth of experience and awareness of the moment, not in physiological flourishes.

No one else was in the cellar. My breathing became shallow. What we wanted was incapable of justification by any of the understandings which had been passed on by our priests, parents, and teachers. If we did it, it would have to be a totally secret act, for punishment would be equally heavy if we were caught. It would be, not because we wanted it so but because it was so given to us, an act of liberation, a blow for freedom of expression.

We mumbled a few words, I don't even remember what we said, and found our way unthinkingly to a dark corner at the very rear of the cellar, where the coal was stored. Rats scuttled in the gloom. I could feel the power of my desire, and the shame which encased it. I pulled my pants down and bent over, putting my palms against the wall. To this day I can remember the texture of the moist crumbling plaster. I closed my eyes and did not know what was going to happen, how it would feel. My knees grew weak with anticipation.

And then the pressure between my buttocks. A sliding sense, a burgeoning warmth, fullness. Something clicked in my mind and I felt pain. Had either of us been more at ease we would have waited a moment until I stretched to accommodate him, and then gone on. But I tensed and panicked, and pulled away. Neither of us moved. I could feel his lust laced with embarrassment. A moment passed.

"I want to fuck you again," he whispered.

My stomach dropped. Often, in reliving the memory, I picture myself whirling about and murmuring "Yes" with my arms curled about him. But I was far from the ability to act so spontaneously. His cock went into me again, and almost before I could adjust to his presence, he came, and pulled out at once.

I sought him out later, wanting to do it again, but he was distant and angry. He had undoubtedly experienced the disgust that those of us raised as Catholics associate with orgasm after so many years of being told how sinful and damaging sex is, how it is an affront to God, and how even touching oneself would land one in the eternal fires of hell. He pushed me away and told me never to bother him again. He was older, bigger, stronger. I was confused and hurt. And my masturbatory fantasies for years were attempts to recapture the moment and bring it to fruition.

The man behind the trucks scratched my head, as one would do to a friendly dog, then zipped up, and sidled off. I stood up and found that all eyes had turned away from me. It was either the height of delicacy or an instantaneous mass attack of indifference in my further behavior.

For the rest of the time I remained there, some five or ten minutes, there was no more "sex." Occasionally one man might rub against another, and a hand would go to someone's genitals, some fondling took place. I thought of the Subud circle, in which no one does anything until the "spirit" is felt. Only, in this case, the thing most often done was a simple physical contact, man touching man. These people were there not merely for sex, but for the freedom to be in a space where sex could take place without unnecessarily elaborate social game playing.

I am aware of the viewpoint which will lament the sadness of men who have to huddle in urine-soaked stone caves to make some brief contact. But surely that perspective has been overdone to the point of tedium. It is time to see even the smallest, most seemingly pitiful action in a new light, the light of human beings who will go to such lengths to maintain *any contact at all*. We have reached the state of repression in this society where we are afraid to touch or be touched, suffocating on our needs and strangling in our inhibitions.

For sexual freedom is not a political movement, not an idea, not a new life style, not an organization. It is the moment-to-moment sensitivity to the fluctuations of the sexual state. And anyone human enough to brave the imprinted taboos, the repressive influences of all society including one's friends, and the very real police danger, ought to understand that the desperation which surrounds sex is due to the times we live in, and does not inhere in the act itself. One wonders how often this must be repeated until one realizes that it is possible to get hooked on guilt, the way a junkie comes to enjoy the penetration of the needle quite independently from the stuff he shoots from it into his arm.

I walked back to the street feeling very high and very solid. The vibration behind me had all the power of a group of men chanting Om. The nature of the small group in front of the car had not changed, although some of the individuals were different. I thought of the difference between these men and those whose rigid hyperheterosexuality results in the misery of a world, and I saw cocksucking from a new perspective.

Getting on our knees is just the way we pray.

Bisexuality, Therapy, and Revolution

These thoughts crystalized during a four-hour period of fucking-meditation at the St. Mark's Baths, a place I visit on the average of once or twice a week for steam and cold plunges, sex, honest conversation, and a species of rumination I find possible in few other environments. I prefer the St. Mark's to the newer, more fashionable baths, partially out of nostalgia, partially out of its historic designation as the birthplace of James Fenimore Cooper, whose ghost haunts the steam room, but also because I have, as a friend once pointed out, "a taste for the seedy."

I went in at eight in the evening holding a single need: to be fucked. I cared for little more than to lie face down on a cot, to stretch out at full length, a pillow under my thighs raising naked buttocks to complete view, and be entered by anywhere from one to twenty men, whose faces I might not even see. I wouldn't leave until I was sated. Nor was I the only man there with such a program in mind. I showered, went to my room, applied a liberal amount of Vaseline to my anus, and flung myself down on the creaky bed, leaving the door open and wondering whether this would be a good night for studs.

Within a few minutes, Lou, one of the attendants, came in. He shut the door behind him and the atmosphere of the room changed immediately. Lou is old school, a fat homely man in his late forties who still refers to gay men as "fags" in a tone not heard since schoolyard days. But I am not prejudiced, especially when my central concern is cock. Also, there is no reason why homosexual encounters must dispense with all elements of perversity. I am not at all certain that the gay militants, in their historically necessary role of changing homosexuals' consciousness, have not insinuated an idealized wholesomeness into the homophile mystique. For myself, I still have a sweet tooth for certain kinds of depravity.

"I'm going to rape you," said Lou, launching into his macho monologue. Since I have discovered that when I assume an overtly passive role it is best to let the active partner set the mood of the intercourse, I complied with his fantasy and allowed myself to imagine myself as a young girl being assaulted by a burly construction worker. I knew enough about Lou and about that kind of mentality in general to realize that his pleasure was dependent on a more complex interaction than simple rape. He needed to imagine that I was at first protesting and then, overwhelmed by his brute masculinity, giving in despite myself. That I was hating myself for enjoying what he was doing to me.

He tied my wrists to the metal headboard with a slip chain and bound my ankles with a strap. He gloated over me for a few minutes. I raised my buttocks and he slapped the cheeks once, very hard. The stinging sensation coupled with the flashing images it provoked ricocheted down the mirrored hallways of my mind, providing a rich and delicious amalgam of annotated feelings. To a large extent, we had become extraneous to one another, for each was fully engrossed in a private scenario which was only incidentally complementary to the other's script.

"I'm going to shove my cock up your ass," he hissed, "and stuff a popper in your nose."

"Good," I thought.

If he had spoken these words in a purely matter-of-fact manner, they would have been categorized as description, but there was a note of accusation in his voice. He at once indicated that what was about to happen was dirty and nasty, and that I was sluttish for wanting it. I thereupon let myself be a slut, an open hole craving penetration. I squirmed on the sheet and tightened my buttocks. It was interesting to play this role of wanton. I knew that if my actions matched his fantasy, he would fuck me with greater force, and to be fucked, you will remember, was my single goal for the evening.

I don't know how many others, men or women, have experienced the desire so cleanly, so simply. The entire social and psychological matrix within which the fucking took place was unimportant; it was the act itself which called me. I strained to raise my buttocks as high as I could and was surprised to hear a whimper of desire escape my lips. I wallowed in voluptuous surrender to the moment.

The question occurred to me: to whom am I surrendering? On the face of it, I was giving myself to him, but a second look revealed that it was to myself that I was yielding. I was giving myself to my own expression. That it emerged as an imitation of a classic image of a lascivious woman was colorful enough, but incidental in terms of meaning. In the midst of my pondering, he mounted me abruptly, having dropped his pants to his knees and not even having bothered to remove his shoes and socks. Added to the other elements, I now had the picture of the partially undressed man lying heavily on the naked body beneath him. It was gloriously whorish.

He raised his pelvis, slid his cock between my thighs, and brought the tip of it to my asshole. With no warning, he burst inside me rudely, I gasped with shock, and my entire body froze, as though I had been impaled on a hook. He gave me no time to relax the sphincter muscle, but began pumping at once, with extreme vigor. Pleasure and pain fought their usual battle, and for perhaps half a minute I disengaged my attention from my feelings and turned to analysis of the sensations between my buttocks. For that space of time I ceased being a voluptuary being fucked and became a psychologist working in the laboratory of lust, registering impressions, cataloguing, structuring.

This had the ancillary effect of allowing enough distraction for my muscles to relax, and I observed that pleasure and pain lost all their connotations and became nothing more than conceptual markers along the total spectrum of undifferentiated sensation. Having accomplished my aim in that area of research, I put aside my charts and switched back to a mode of non-critical appreciation of what was happening.

What Lou lacked in subtlety he made up for in strength. I felt his thighs thrashing against the backs of my legs, his arms wrapped tightly around my chest, his cock hard and imperative, charging the tender tissues of my analogue cunt. I dove into a mindless state, relinquishing all control, all responsibility, and experienced the lazy enjoyment of voluntary bondage. I needed to do nothing but let him use me as a pillow for his ride. He cared only that I act as victim, and that freed me to have my feelings in private. I wondered how many women waste so much time blaming a man for what he doesn't give them instead of learning to enjoy what he is capable of?

His chatter was criminally inane. "You like that, don't you?" he kept saying. At first I heard the bravado, the necessity of the male to assert himself. But after a bit I could detect the whine of insecurity that hummed beneath it. It is a commonplace observation that to the degree a person pushes the ambience of a scene, to that degree he is uncertain of himself within that scene. I became aware that Lou's breathing was shallow, that he was holding himself rigidly against me. I momentarily despaired at being in the arms of such an uptight lover, but I dipped beneath that to find a hint of compassion. So often in the past, when I had struggled with myself in the embrace of a woman, I had been met with contempt. And I contrasted that to the times when a woman continued to give of herself, despite my fears and clumsiness, and how much I came to care for the simple human warmth involved in that.

Realizing that it was senseless to condemn, I pushed back and pressed my buttocks into him, splitting myself apart on his cock, hanging my fleshy weight on that insistent pole. Only those who have experienced that particular sensation will know the breath-stopping wonder of it. I ground my hips around, contracted my cheeks, and pushed my anus out. This was the second part of the scenario: the rapist's victim contacts her own desire and begins to respond.

At that point he snapped the ampule of amyl nitrate and held it to my nostrils. The sixty seconds of whirring began, the amplification of contact, the giddy descent into sensitized helplessness.

"Oh you fuck, you little bitch, you cunt!" he said, and climaxed inside me, his whole torso clenched in a single orgasmic spasm. There were none of the flowing melting rippling feelings which mark the orgasm of a relaxed man. This was a sniggering come, a lonely guilt-ridden ejaculation. I accepted it and then sagged onto the bed.

He stood up quickly, wiping his cock on the edge of the sheet, pulled up his pants, and untied me. We did not exchange another word. After he left, I lay back, throbbing, and thought about what had just happened in relation to what was taking place between myself and two women who had served as focal points for my emotional existence during the previous year and a half. The energy coursing through me had gone first and foremost to my brain.

Maureen was twenty-four, extremely sensual, with a keen analytic mind. She could lie for hours and let herself be stroked and licked. Her fucking was of two basic kinds: shallow, leading to orgasm, and deep, without orgasm. Seventy percent of our sex involved the second type, in which she would lie on her back, kick her legs to the ceiling, clutch her ankles in her hands, and let her cunt go slack, allowing me to prod, caress, slosh, shake, penetrate, and in general do anything I wished in relation to that gaping organ. At such times her experience was so intense that she uttered not a sound. When she wanted to come, on the other hand, she would lie with her legs fairly close together, her eyes closed, her forehead furrowed, while I moved steadily, in and out, pausing at certain cyclical check points, varying pitch, angle, and intensity. Her climb to climax was as obvious as the line of a fever chart, and she kept absolute control over her excitement, holding the thread, until the very last moment when, with deep moans and twitches, she reached some kind of physiological convulsion. There was never any blending of the two modes.

Elaine was the counterpart. Thirty-five, gently cynical, she cared little for preliminaries and liked to get right down to the coupling of cock and cunt. Once inside her, a current connected us, and I didn't have to do anything except follow its directives. Neither of us moved very much externally; all the flow was within. We could lie quite still and feel the mountain wave seize us both, and only had to remain sensitive to its curl, like surf riders, to have it bring us to climax. With her I reached many orgasms of feeling before ejaculating, and usually she would have come five or six times by then. The fucking was oddly cerebral without being intellectual, animal without being brutal.

The scene I had with them went through three stages: living with Elaine, living with Maureen, and then living with Elaine again while still seeing Maureen. I thought the third would be ideal, but found that it required immense energy to sustain both relationships, especially since neither of them wanted to have anything to do with the other. Maureen was involved in some women's liberation coven and was forever talking about her "sisters" and the need for women to help one another. But when I asked her to call Elaine, so that the two of them might close the circuit of the triangle and relieve me of the burden of trying to lead two distinct lives, she welled with hostility and jealousy. I was torn between two women, each of whom said she cared for me, but who were unwilling to translate that affection into an effort to ease the split I felt within me. It was simply another example of how people get involved in the rigamarole of political organizations, digest the rhetoric, and yet, when it comes time to apply their ideology to the problems of everyday life—which is, after all, the only life we have—revert to atavistic patterns. I was backed by their intransigence into a hateful role, having to articulate preference and make a choice.

The next man walked into my room. He was black, soft, tall, with luminous eyes and deep lips. His cock was almost eight inches long. He entered me from in front, his mouth covering mine as he did, and I opened to him easily, sensing that his approach was one of tenderness. A nice contrast to what had gone before. It is only at the baths that such chiaroscuro is possible. I was pleased that I was able to accommodate such a large cock so easily, and mused that Lou's power tactics had served a useful purpose besides having their own value.

"This is so good, so good," said my new lover. "Your pussy is so open, so wide, this is so good." And indeed it was. I rose to him and stretched my legs to receive him more deeply. I let him have me utterly, without reservation. Even when he prodded the sensitive prostate gland, it was softly, and I knew he wouldn't hurt me, so I could let him have even that intimacy, the sensations of which drove me to a fenzy of moaning. I nuzzled his throat and ran my hands over his hard shoulders, down his slender back, over his firm buttocks. This was the fucking I had come for. I felt lucky that I had scored so soon.

The question which arose at this point was: what was my motivation for leaving my apartment late in the evening to trek the wasteland of Eighth Street and climb the salty stairs of the crusty St. Mark's Baths in order to have a stranger split my buttocks with his anonymous erection?

Several answers presented themselves in rapid order: I was working out some childhood trauma, I was following the call of an obsession, I was hungry for sensation, I was balancing the yin of living with a woman with enough yang to keep me in sexual perspective. I turned my attention to the central focus of the act: the cock sliding in and out of the asshole. Those who have not been anally fucked will have only words to guide them, and those who have may not have entered into introspection while it was going on. In either case, the difficulty of describing the thing is immense, for it stimulates associative areas of the brain which bring to life a terribly complex and intensely personal web of memories and insights.

There is a burning sweetness (remember the enemas my mother used to give), a feeling of fullness (remember the first time I was fucked, at fifteen, in the cellar, and when his cock went into me I couldn't catch my breath), a tenderness deep inside (recall the mornings lying in bed thinking of the scene in the movie Tom Sawyer where one boy rescues another from drowning and they lie on the bank, wet, spent, lolling in one another's arms), a melting and a running (the overwhelming sense of relief when you race the attack of diarrhea to the john and get there just in time to let the brown fluid spurt into the bowl).

My cheeks nestled into the hollows of his thighs, our legs kicked and intertwined, and overall was the giving of myself, the offering of my ass on the altar of fucking. The fantasies and images, with which Lou had me as a dirty teenage girl, now showed me as a rugged woman in the arms of her man. I felt possessive of my lover at that moment, and sucked him into me. It was my body giving him pleasure, it was my body that supported him. And through him, I gained an identity of loving.

He fucked me until he came, and his orgasm was full and rippling, a pulsating shooting into my flesh, a throbbing and a dribbling into my bowels. And when it was over, he lay on me a long time, letting his breathing return to normal. This was a *man* above me, and I was a *man*. And yet all my sense of self cried out that I was a woman. We shared a cigarette and the poignant awareness that we would probably never meet again, for there was a tacit understanding that neither of us would pursue an attempt at repetition. In the baths, the quality of fleetingness, sometimes as delicate as the nuance in a Japanese watercolor, permeates all meetings and suffuses them with intimations of the human tragedy.

Perhaps then I should have quit and returned home. Yet, I was not surprised that while I had got what I came for, that wasn't the end of the story. I no longer *needed* to get fucked; now I *wanted* to get fucked. And that introduced a new element into my condition.

Is it only a man getting fucked in the ass who wants more? Shouldn't this be even more the case with a woman being fucked in the cunt, the organ that was specifically evolved for that activity? How many times had I lain in the arms of a woman after several hours of fucking, feeling her still churning under me, the fires of her passion only just beginning to burn, and I with a limp cock, depleted after two or three ejaculations? Usually they had been properly conditioned, and smothered their frustration, especially in the light of the fact that I had performed far and beyond any reasonable expectation. I am not now speaking of emotional satisfaction, but of physiological completion, and of psychic yearning for ever higher planes of ecstasy. Isn't it at just such a moment that the next shift, so to speak, should take over and proceed with her to the subsequent peak?

Six more men came in during the next hour and each fucked me according to his merit. The experiences ranged from the insignificant to the profound. There came a point at which my perimeters melted and I became pure malleable flesh. I wore many masks during that time, both in physical positions and in inner attitudes. And knew that I was entering a deep flow of energy when I began to feel cold liquid flashes up my spine, the surest sign that my deepest muscular tensions were melting.

The tender tissues of the anus, however, began to protest, and once again pain gained ascendancy over pleasure. This triggered a new train of images. Now I was the eternal victim, suffering for the gratification of others, an erotic Christ giving myself up to satisfy the single-pointed need of the hungry men who passed by my door. I entered the space of the holy degenerate, the kingdom of Genet, and was transmogrified into the person whose very disintegration and degradation liberates the energy to raise others up. The scene assumed dimensions of depravity, a sadomasochistic peanut butter and jelly sandwich, with each increasingly excruciating penetration of cock giving rise to notions of saintliness. The wicked and the sublime were at one another's throats, and as I let out growls of animal power, as I lifted my ass higher and higher, coming at last to my knees to offer the rounded and vulnerable rump to the marauding cock, I was as blessed as any believer receiving a communion wafer on his tongue. Only instead of the mumbo jumbo of some sleepy habitualized priest, I had the song of my own awareness to transform my carnal desires into hosannas of praise, my flesh into spirit.

But here, the words of my therapist intruded. She is a bioenergeticist in the line of Lowen and Pierrakos, although her basic tool is sensitivity to the condition of the other through the reverberations she receives in herself. We had been dealing with the question of pain, using her observation that I seemed to possess some sort of psychic switch which, at high levels of interaction, throws the tracks toward the area of self-destruction. "A propensity for negativity" she called it, and once it had been named, I could see quite clearly how it operated. Her way of working involved less interest in the historical roots of trauma than in their actual immediate structure and functioning, and we did not go deeply into the possible events which might have brought about my current state of affairs. It was obvious that masochism could be translated into psychological terms as a need to be punished, an expiation of guilt, a repetition compulsion, and so forth. But none of that would help me to locate, in my present psychophysiological structure, the nature and location of the switch. She went, therefore, directly into the musculature, into the breathing, and into the feelings.

I wondered, as the man above me rode my rump, whether I could learn something about why I seemed to swing toward the pain portion of the spectrum. I put my attention of the hurt that assailed my asshole. I asked myself what I was doing to hurt myself. I found that I was subtly constricting the sphincter muscles. What would happen if I let go? Immediately the sensation of shitting arose. The cock became a turd. Could I expel it? I pushed out. The cock slid back. I relaxed. The cock slid in. It was like loading a rifle.

At once I was taken with a realization of my morbid fear of letting anyone see me shit. "Ah Freud!" I thought, "thou art with us yet." The whole question of the way body functions are sectioned off in our culture stung me with full force. And in a breathtaking leap, I saw that the one thing which probably bound the entire political spectrum together, from right to left, was a feces phobia that marked everyone a closet anal retentive. I had rediscovered the lowest common denominator of American civilization.

I remembered the first time I had been rimmed and the man under me had asked me to shit in his mouth. I was shocked to the point of being sickened. Over the years, however, especially since I had come to terms with my own urge to have that done to me, I saw that coprophiliacs, while suffering from an abysmally low self-esteem, were probably the only people who had the courage to face, in total depth, the primitive taboo that binds us all and which, once broken, is revealed as little more than a function of communication and curiosity. It was one of the first clues to the formulation I later made: that what is called perversion is the most useful map for understanding the true nature of fascism and *the most potent means to unlocking its hold upon us.*

I hold firmly with Reich that the political and military aspects of fascism are the superstructural manifestations of the rigidity of the character formation of the individuals who live in, that is to say, constitute, a fascist state. The enemy is within our own bodies. This is not to deny the economic brutality of the corporate state and the effect it has of perpetuating the crime of civilizing babies. It is only to state that the person who blows up the bank must also be able to eat shit. For if the entire capitalist/imperialist complex of industry, military, education, and government which is our official America were to be wiped out by masses of radicals, unless those radicals had previously freed themselves of their internal armor they would be absolutely unable to form any sort of society which was not repressive. For they themselves would be repressed, and repressed people cannot live together in freedom.

The Vaseline melted from the heat of friction, the feces ran out of the hole, spilling down my buttocks, over my thighs. The room filled with a sour smell. I spread my legs. I let myself shit freely.

"Oh beautiful, baby," said the man above me. "Make it like that, just make it like that."

His cock soared like a great bird in fight, swooping in from all angles, plunging easily, rising softly. His pelvis whipped about on oiled hinges as the energy coursed through him, and I lay at his pleasure, no longer afraid of what might pour out of me. I rejoiced in his joy. Who he was, what his name or personal history were, did not matter. He was man, he was human, he was me. It was the working out of the process that was important, not the personalities involved. I wondered what was going on in his mind, whether he too was in the throes of some great realization, or whether his brain had become a seething center of formless symbols.

A deep soothing warmth spread through my bowels, as though my colon had been given a Vicks rub. Had the imperative to fuck ultimately been issued from my intestines, I wondered, an order from my organic intelligence, which my conditioned mind had then to rationalize as best it could? Anything I could think about what I was doing paled to utter insignificance before the liberating effect of actually doing it. My body was speaking, demanding what it needed.

This returned me to another aspect of the bioenergetic therapy I was involved in, one in which the function of vomiting was explored. At times I would drink glasses of warm salty water and stick a finger down my throat until I threw up, the notion being to loosen the tension in my stomach and chest, and return me to the times when I was force-fed, either food or instruction or "mother love." On those nights I went into the baths not primarily to be fucked, but to suck cock, I often pushed the cock into my throat until I gagged and sometimes vomited. I would find that the cock had become a breast and the semen was the milk I was sucking for. The ambivalence was clear in the contradictory act of sucking for more, and then throwing up because I had had too much.

This is, by the way, not an attempt at reductionism, but a plea for understanding that the sexual act, in all its forms, has many layers of motivation. It was, for example, only when I realized and admitted that the cock in my mouth was also a substitute for the breast I had had as an infant, that I could truly accept the cock as a cock. After I said to myself, "All right, I am sucking cock to relive the days of breastfeeding," I was free to ask, "Given that, do I still want to suck cock or not?" For to understand the roots of a phenomenon is not necessarily to rob the phenomenon of its own integrity. This is why therapy does not "cure" homosexuality. And this is the error in Janov's erroneous contention that healthy people cannot be homosexuals. After all the symbolic, or neurotic, mainsprings of the homosexual act have been plumbed, and the person has attained to complete wholeness, the choice of homosexuality then becomes free and conscious, instead of based on unmet needs.

To suck a cock, and have it be a breast, a finger, a urine tube, an impregnator, and the sexual organ of another human being, to accept the experience on all its levels, is one of the most truly aesthetically and sensually pleasing activities there is. To be able to use the act as a therapeutic tool is an added dimension usually overlooked.

After the man who had willy-nilly witnessed the liberation of my fecal inhibitions left, I went to the bathroom to clean up a bit, and found that I was bleeding. Some tissue had been torn, and that seemed to end fucking for the night. I returned to my room, lay down again, on my back, and began to massage my cock. I did it in a way that might have looked, in the dark, like a woman fingering her cunt. I have explored, but not yet understood, this aspect of my homosexual behavior. The act is generally most satisfying when I work with the image of my being a woman, although when I am in a more involved relationship with a man, I discard all imagery altogether. In this case, the image is like a microscope, merely an instrument with which to examine the subject more minutely.

It had taken some time to distinguish between the male/female model as against the active/passive model. It was with Maureen that I had been able, for the first time, to be both male and passive, lying in total acceptance as she squatted over me and straddled my cock with her cunt. Prior to that, with a woman, I had always had to *do* something, pump my pelvis or fondle her breasts or be actively thinking. It was a delight to give it all up to her, my eyes closed, my breathing regular, almost as though I were napping, while she worked herself up to a frenzy over me. Her cunt moved in a score of ways, her ass jiggling, her hips grinding. It was then that my four basic functional images became clear: active male, passive male, active female, passive female.

Thus I could lie as a woman in the baths, prodding my cock to erection, all the while sending out vibrations of wanting to be aggressed upon. The combination seems to be irresistible. There is something about the sight of a woman-with-an-erection that draws men in by the dozens.

That night they began to come in as I pulled my cock and rolled my head from side to side and flicked my tongue around in my open mouth and kicked my legs on the bed. Independent of any relation to anyone else, I was transported with the power of expression. I let all the restrained gestures of a repressive civilization fall away, and exulted in letting my body find its own language of delight. I was blessed with legions of fantastic revelations, drawn from mythology and the jungle. I was rediscovering the difference between expression and communication, and finding the liberation in unfettered signalling, not caring who read the messages or how they were interpreted.

I thought of how fascism manifests itself in the posture and movements of a people, how we become straight, tight, restricted. How the boundless happiness and profundity of the dance is denied us. We spend almost all our waking hours shuffling about like robots, limited to a paltry handful of expressions, mostly the artificial smile, the unconscious frown, and the bland face. Ancient societies, understanding that civilization is intrinsically inhibiting, had escape valves for repressed energies. In our adolescent America, the only orgies we enjoy are football games and massing together electronically to watch phallic rockets plunge into the womb of the moon. I reasoned that if my culture allowed no orgies in the street, forbid naked bodies to roll about gleaming in the night, I would hold a one-man orgy, and invite all who wanted to come as spectators or participants.

I lost count of how many walked into the room. Some were confused and didn't know what to do with themselves in relation to me. They left quickly, after a few vague caresses. The ones who saw that I was tripping out on my own and didn't care what was done to me, very soon came to put their cocks in my mouth, letting me suck and lick them. I took what came so long as it did not interfere with my inner rhythm. Different shapes, different sizes, different colors. A number reached climax and time and again the slippery jism spurted on my tongue, on my lips, in my throat, until I reeked with sperm.

With each one of them—and at one point two men knelt at either side of me and filled my mouth with both their cocks—I brought myself to the very edge of ejaculation, letting the energy of my impending orgasm feed the movements of my body and the excitement of my lips and tongue. The closer I came to ejaculation, the more frantically I sucked. I twisted my legs, I rolled my torso, I was the epitome of every pornographic fantasy realized.

And then the sounds began, the bubbling noises from my chest. At first they seemed like cries of sexual excitement, but I soon recognized them as moans of despair, sobs of sadness. They were the groanings of a person who was at his last. It occurred to me that I was at the brink of a breakthrough into a feeling I had long been hiding from myself, and as I examined my inner space, tears sprang to my eyes and I began to weep. Sorrow swept through me, liberating a legion of memories, an army of insights. Portions of my self which I had not been in contact with sprang forth to complete new gestalten of understanding. This was the sorrow that the pain was a defense against, and I saw that the sorrow was itself a longing for all the unfulfilled dreams of a lifetime. I yearned for the truth and beauty and union I had known instinctively as a child, and then had systematically and brutally beaten from me by the insane conditioning of the fiendish civilization into which I had been born. The entire process of dehumanization which is the keynote of the ugly edifice of our cultured world, this culture which has deified the machine, and worships power and greed and lying above all that is simple and noble and elegant in life. The whole picture flashed clearly and I sobbed for the loss of all that was good, as the cock pulsed and spat its acrid juices into my trembling mouth.

"Am I really a degenerate?" I thought, "or is it that I have the courage to find a mode of expression where others might just succumb to becoming grey automatons in the system?"

I formulated the notion that this was the essence of revolution: the realization that one has had one's humanity robbed by the civilization one lives in, and the effort to break through the conditioning to some fullness of expression, no matter what form it takes, whether it is fighting at the barricades or wallowing in orgy houses. And upon that I saw that such a process could not be separated from therapy, or rather, the therapeutic ambience, which involves seeing and experiencing the ways in which the evils of the civilization are built into our very character structure.

I remembered all my encounters with so-called revolutionary groups, recalling that my disillusionment with them was based on a single fact: that every one of them had begun as an impetus toward freedom of expression and ended as another mode of conformity. And the reason was always the same: the inability to accept that we carry the ills of the culture within ourselves. And the battle to overthrow the old order begins there. And sooner or later in this struggle, we come upon the realm of sex, and find ourselves face to face with The Perversions. And who has the courage to pass through those doors, while owning the intelligence to understand exactly what it is that is being passed through?

One last man came into the room, and he looked at me once and pierced through my gyrations to see the person that I am. He closed the door, locking us into a state of intimacy, took me in his arms, kissed me, and crooned in my ear. His hands caressed my buttocks and his cock entered my bleeding asshole. We fucked for a very long time and I wondered what it all meant, that I should be brought to physical damage, emotional convolution, and intellectual skydiving, in order to enjoy this simple embrace.

The many strands of the dilemma wove themselves in and out around a single perception, starting with the possibility that we ultimately be no more than tools for one another's masturbation, no matter what rationalization we employ. I was reminded of the times I lay lapping a woman's cunt and glancing up to see her licking her lips and running her hands over her breasts, revelling in her own sensations. A woman surrenders herself to beauty to the degree that a man is strong enough to refrain from trying to conquer her. He must follow his own arc of excitement, sensitive to her responses, and if all goes well will be graced with the most exquisite of experiences, the unutterable opening of another soul.

Afterward, the man and I talked, disclosing something of the details of our lives. "It took so many years," I said, "to find out why I let men fuck me. Under all the jargon, concurrent with the hunger for pain and degradation, hand in hand with every single combination and permutation of thought and feeling, runs a single truth: *like it*." Shades of Lou's frantic chant went through my mind. "You like it, don't you," he always accused. And it was as simple as that, once the symbolic garbage had been thrown away. I had explored sex through its many estuaries, seen all the psychodynamic and political ramifications, and emerged with a single small understanding: I liked it.

Is that so hideous a thing that it should be so difficult to discover? It would not seem so, but in the face of the evidence I must conclude that almost everyone and everything I have met in my life has conspired to deny me the right to enjoy being fucked in the ass. Might not, I extrapolated, it be the same for a woman? Might she not suffer the same problem about being fucked in the cunt? Does a woman have to struggle against the conscious and unconscious conditioning which has trained her to view the slit between her legs as something drastically nasty?

I lept from my therapist's words to the effect that our slavery is locked in our bodies to the realization that all historical repression has served one end: to keep the individual human being from doing what he or she *pleases*, to the point of actually destroying the capability of people to experience pleasure. And while we are familiar with the obvious forms of this repression, such as economic inequality, and racist suppression, and outright police control, we often miss that it is built into the human personality from birth, through the media of official religions, educational systems, governmental structures, and all the paraphernalia of social convention, beginning with the nuclear family.

I took a deep breath and pulled in the pungent smells of the room: sweat, sperm, shit, Vaseline, tobacco. The American obsession with cleanliness came to mind, and I saw that our fascism is insidiously undermining our very senses. The deodorants, the vaginal sprays, the air fresheners, the ammonia-laced soaps, all conspire to destroy the importance of the sense of smell. Smell, the most directly perceived of all the senses, must be kept alive, pertinent, or else the individual is dulled. For a person or a people to be free, their senses must be vibrant. To destroy the senses is to destroy the person. The primitive dictatorship of the Nazis was child's play, I saw, compared to the sophisticated destruction of freedom by American industry and its smirking lackey, Madison Avenue. The very means by which we perceive the world are being attacked. Fascism has less to do with guns than it does with robotism.

The man left, and I wondered what had been accomplished. Another night of fucking, another grabbing of insights, another display of expression. And to what end? I had experienced a momentary personal liberty, my mind had pierced through another layer of lies. But in the nation and the world at large, it was growing darker. It is the same as it has been through all recorded history: the masters rule and the slaves respond. And both are caught in the deadlines of their empty lives, the rigidity of their desensitized bodies. The major difference is that in America, which has been systematically robbing the rest of the world of its wealth while destroying an entire continent in the name of progress, even the peons can have automobiles. We use stolen resources to make the lollipops which distract us from the need for real food. We are implicated every time we (for example) use a typewriter to write a piece denouncing the system.

The existence of government, any government, is proof that the people of that place are not free. The free human being does not look to another for answers to the meaning of life and does not need organized education or hierarchical religion. The free human being will not be taxed or told when to go to war. Free people come together to accomplish some task, to plant a field, to build a house, to make a baby, to face an enemy, to share in the high vibrations of communion. Any relationship which persists past the accomplishing of its initial purpose is the ground upon which fascism flourishes. This includes everything from the Catholic Church and the Communist Party, to ersatz radical groups whose first accomplishment is to construct a subculture which apes the system of the society it claims to be overthrowing, to marriages which go on as horrid shells of a former dream.

I went again to the showers, washed, returned to my room, and dressed. As I was putting on my clothes, another man looked in. It was a sexy moment. My pants were halfway up my legs, my buttocks still exposed. It was possible to go one more round. And then it was as though I was looking down an endless corridor. I could stay there and be fucked until I starved to death. Why do that? Why not? I remained in indecision until he tired of my static pose and walked away. The choice had, temporarily, been made for me. I collected my effects from the desk and walked outside.

It was a little after midnight. In the street, the cops, the speed freaks, the hoods, the heads, the people passing through, the shopkeepers, the dogs, the children, the roaches, the garbage, presented a single vision of the state of our civilization. It was Downtown Kali Yuga, the lowest point in the history of the species. It was also, I remembered, the Age of Aquarius, the chance for global renaissance. Which way would the pointer fall? Further descent into slavery and ultimate destruction, or individual awakening and the birth of free expression? Walking home I looked at the people who passed, and no one seemed awake. Each was locked in some private prison called the armored body. I had no hope that enough would wake up in time. I could not conceive of any of them able to explore the roots of their condition, to do the hard work necessary to effect a transformation from a destruction-oriented band of apes to rational animals which affirm life.

I went home and drank whiskey until unconsciousness stole over my brain.

Beyond Bisexuality

I

Lucinda and Gerard

We flowed through the ancient choreography of desire. We did nothing that has not been done through the millenia of recorded history and into the unwritten hundreds of thousands of years before our species began to take itself seriously enough to begin recording its folly. The changes from one configuration to the next were so organic that there was no sense of separation between positions. Moving like dancers in notation, still all our actions were spontaneous.

I sucked his cock while she sucked mine . . . he took my cock into his mouth while she swallowed his . . . she lapped at my cock while he tongued her cunt . . . she received both our cocks between her lips at the same time . . .

The catalogue is lengthy, listing most of the variations possible among three people. The moment of highest focus came as he fucked me from behind while I was fucking her from in front. I felt her cunt clasp my cock as his cock slid between my buttocks. The sensation was like peaking on acid.

She later talked about the experience in ecstatic terms, describing the overpowering excitement of having two men pour their energy into her. He said it was the single most erotic moment of his lifetime. For me, it was the bridging of a deep inner schism. The twin element of my being fused: mother and father joined in my consciousness as once their egg and sperm had joined to create that consciousness.

My pelvis rolled and buttocks flexed in response to his entry, and the concurrent circling of my cock triggered the mounting tension in her to a surging orgasm. As I then went with the rhythms of her tumultuous eruption, he burst into climax. I was drawn by the vortex of total sharing of myself among the three of us, and when I came, the vibrations were those of us all.

I had been in scores of threesomes, but it was either me fucking two women, or another man and myself fucking a single woman, or three men together. This was the first time I attained to complete relationship to both a man and a woman simultaneously and equally. It resulted in a unification of perspective that introduced the contradictory aspects of my being to one another without the comforting buffer of confusion, and forced me to face the fragmentation of my soul.

During the course of the night, I was also alone with each of them at different times.

She and I talked, whispering, holding hands, our foreheads almost touching, while he went to another part of the house to be by himself. It mattered little what we said, the tales were told. It was the communion that transported us, the intimacy. When we fucked, it was by falling gently from words into deeds, deepening the bond between us.

Later, with him, there was a closeness of a comparable kind. I found myself in a mood of narcissistic responsiveness, and as he stood over me, I became passive, soft. I cared for little but to float in an onanistic reverie, allowing my body to find its own arcane expressions of yielding. He could use me as he wished, so long as he was content to remain solitary. He put himself in proportion to my state and found his pleasure by acting the complement to my desire. As I closed my eyes and stretched lazily, I thought of how deliciously it contrasted to other times with men, when I would be fiercely active, and give myself with yearning pelvis and wild cries of need.

Before dawn, as we all slept, I lost all distinctions, lying between the two of them. There seemed to be no difference in our sexes. I was not a man, nor was I a woman, but something which included both. And like any good gestalt, I was greater than the sum of my parts.

II

Robert and Diane

With the energy born of exploration, we worked our way through a Kama Sutra kaleidoscope. The costumes of our insights and the import of our revelations were but varied aspects of a single awareness: the reverberation of cosmic vibration through the medium of the human body.

He entered her tenderly from behind, swelling between her buttocks, and I entered her cunt from in front. For a dazzling arc out of time we rang in all the changes of feeling possible in that position. I had my arms around his shoulders, his mouth pressed to mine, as she writhed between us, caught on our cocks, taking us in and giving to us all at once.

We followed no programme, and yet I found a path through a vast array of complex interlockings. Most poignantly I remember her lips against mine, our kiss hot with passion, while his cock throbbed like a third tongue between our own.

Again I was fucked while fucking. She lay under me in classic pose, her legs at a thirty degree angle, her knees slightly raised, as I swam in the hot moistness of her cunt easily. Suddenly, he was on top of me and with a stuttering shudder his cock soared between my buttocks and penetrated my flesh. As he moved into the privacy of my inner space of sensation, the basic question of all bisexuality came to the surface: how to be a man to the woman while being a woman to the man, and how to be a man to the woman while being a man to the man, and how to be a woman to the woman while being a woman to the man, and how to be a woman to the woman while being a man to the man?

I could not deal, with the multiplicity of levels except by surrender, and at that, the patterns began to sort themselves out. For awhile, each thrust of his cock was matched by a pulsation of light in her eyes. Each roll of her pelvis and sigh from her chest was encased in the stillness of his mind and mine as they interpenetrated and became one consciousness to behold the beauty of the woman between us. Our hands found each other, and in the mingling of fingers I could no longer tell which was his, which hers, which mine, which was right, which was left. Like trapeze artists, we had lept from our perches of safety and found ourselves given up to trust and timing.

The open manifestation of the bifurcation within me brought forth the split within each of them, and at a stroke, we were six. The shifts were rapid and startling. In one moment we were two men and a woman, and then became three men, and again, three women, changing into two men and a man. The genital realities played tag with the psychic states. The subtleties ramified. The man in me was not only a straight male responding as such to a female, and a gay male responding as such to a male, but also a male lesbian swooning in exquisite ambiguity between the figures on either side.

Finally, our breathing synchronized. Our inhalations and exhalations magnified so that each breath had the power of three, increasing the energy available to us to a superhuman capacity.

We did something that went even further to nourish the metamorphosis. I lay on my back, him sucking me while I kissed her. It was as though I were delineated at the waist. My lower part was male and my upper part was female. I kissed her as a woman kisses a woman and she caressed my breasts while he sucked me as a man sucks a man. A sudden shift, and I was a man from the waist up while a woman below. Now I was a man kissing a woman while feeling the sweet melting of my woman's body to his male mouth.

With a buzzing connection, the male and female inside me began to undulate in a series of sine waves. I lost my sexual *identity* and became a sexual *entity*. Yet, there was none of the out-of-focus loss of sense of self that often accompanies experiences of that kind. On the physical plane, I had a sure awareness of myself as a gen-itally male animal; I knew my name; I remembered the nature of things. Reality was pervasive.

Then, a sense of urgency, a quickening of the life force, a deeper pulsation. Inside, male and female had fused; outside, male and female pressed upon me. We all crept in closer, we began to make sounds, we wept at the scope of the orgasm that swept toward us.

During the ensuing ecstasy, all the centers of my being operated independently and harmoniously. The instinctual brain moved my body, as the emotive core sent bolts of yearning through my system; I raised my arms to the heavens. The intellectual center was caught in a state of wordless wonder at the fact of existence, and the higher faculties spun mighty mandalas of meaning.

Through it all, my eyes opened and looked upon the brute truth of the actual room we lay in, saw the flickering shadows on the ceiling thrown by the candle next to the bed, and I heard from the stereo at the far corner of the room, the Beatles singing, "In my life I loved you more."

III

Sex is a key to doorways of knowing. For me it has been a yoga through which new qualities of self evolved. Like the alchemist who works with a potion for decades and in the process brings about a transmutation of his essence, I spent all my conscious life since the age of eight mixing elements in the crucible of sex, sifting enormous amounts of material to produce a few grams of pure substance. I had fucked or been fucked by over five hundred different women, and twice that many men, in circumstances ranging from brief gaspings in alleys and whorehouses to lengthy relationships. I had gone through all the possible scenarios. And with the suddenness of total change, I became a different kind of person.

At the far edge of bisexuality I realized that all that had gone before was but the task of perfecting the instrument, the mindbody that is myself. My adventures had served a single purpose: to exhaust all the subjective aspects of the sexual act. The many modes, which had been challenges, areas of exploration, were now my tools—homosexuality, heterosexuality, bisexuality, abstruse psychosexual states and practices, the so-called perversions, the many masks of libidinal displacement . . .

these were now at my command, to be used the way a director uses a cast of characters to realize a vision.

Having no term which encompassed the totality of my erotic awareness and function, I found it necessary to coin a new word, and thus formulated the concept: METASEXUALITY.

IV

Metasexual consciousness is born once one has healed the internal male-female duality. Strictly speaking, only those who have attained that state are capable of understanding it. But in the same way that the Buddha nature inheres in every living thing, and enlightenment is simply a waking up to what we have been all along, metasexuality is manifested in all human beings whether they know it or not. But to see this involves at least an intellectual effort, that of making the distinction between metasex and sex itself.

Sex is that activity which takes places between one man and one woman who are fucking to make a baby. Metasex is everything else. This is gone into in full detail in The Metasexual Manifesto, so I won't elaborate here. In this essay, I would like only to suggest some of what is uncovered once that crucial distinction is made. For once we cease applying the laws of sex to metasex, metasex reveals itself as a rich and unexplored territory.

The most blatant example of confusion between the two vehicles lies at the core of every historical civilization—and a metasexual awakening challenges this principle head on—and consists of the prejudice that *two* is the *natural* number for the erotic encounter. This is obviously valid for the sexual realm but proves completely erroneous in the metasexual worldview. The assumption that *two* allows the most perfect erotic union is a misconception rooted in primitive bisexual consciousness.

When one transcends male-female dualism, eroticism becomes suceptible of a more subtle mathematical understanding. For each number, there is a different and unique quality of consciousness, and no one is intrinsically superior to any of the others.

One, the single point, metasex of no dimension. This is the realm of masturbation, that poorly understood activity, usually considered to be an aberration, but actually a powerful vehicle in its own right. To masturbate to full orgasm (not merely ejaculation or clitoral twitching, but full vegetative release) is a sublime and solitary act, requiring capacity for fear and awe. To bring about one's own orgasm, without the company of others, without fantasies to mask the facticity of the deed, requires great inner resources.

One has certain shadings, for a person can masturbate in the presence of others and vary the nature of the experience. Masturbating while another assists, giving positive reinforcement, kissing, stroking, speaking, is a profound means of grasping the reality of self and other. How many couples, thinking themselves uninhibited, are unable to masturbate in one another's presence? It is not going too far to suggest that unless an individual has come to terms with *one*, he or she will lack full capability in the higher numbers.

Two is the official sexual model of our civilization, entrenched in our archtypal mind. It is, however, from a metasexual viewpoint, nothing more than the metasex of a single line, the metasex of one dimension: it is totally flexible since a line can assume an infinity of curves, but it always remains in one dimension.

A ———————————————→ **B**

With *two* accepted as the ideal, the "natural" way of doing things, the other numbers get relegated to the categories of sin, crime, perversion, or diversion. Even many sophisticates measure their orgies against an unconscious norm. Again, this is because they have not dealt with the internal bisexual split.

The enforced exclusivity of the number even damages the couple-form itself. As people try to squeeze all erotic exploration into that single format, it suffers from a fatal overload. It is as though, with the integral calculus available to us, a law was passed forbidding us to do anything but count on our fingers and toes.

Two has its uses, its value, and its delights, as well as its limitation. Biologically, it is the vehicle of procreation. And it possesses a certain classic purity of line which makes it attractive to radicals as well as traditionists. Perhaps its major appeal lies in its comparative simplicity.

Three is the first number in the metasex of two dimensions, metasex of the plane. *Three* must be understood as more than the addition of one more to the basic two. It involves a whole new quality of consciousness, something which cannot come about with people who are still thinking in male-female terms.

The fact of the new dimension becomes clear when one sees that within a triangle, the twosome is but one element of the greater vehicle. In a triangle, in fact, there are seven elementary constituent parts:

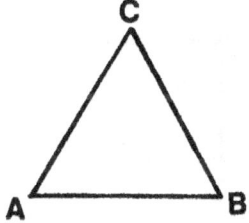

individuals: A, B, C; couples: AB, AC, BC; and the overall form: ABC.

In theory, the triangle is equilateral; in practice, there are many functional variations. For example, using the situation with Robert and Diane, with Robert as A, Diane as B, and myself as C, Robert and Diane, a mated pair-bond, represent a stronger energy than either Robert and myself or Diane and myself; thus, AB will be shorter than either AC or BC. But that is only within one category. Since Diane and I are in a pair-formation situation in terms of our biological sexuality, our metasex will have an intensity greater than what happens between her and Robert in the pair-maintenance situation. In this triangle, BC will be shorter than either AB or AC. In a third context, since Robert and I have cocks and Diane a cunt, the AC bond will possess an idiosyncratic quality which neither AB or BC can manifest, thus giving yet another shape to the basic triangle.

It is possible to go on, showing how differences in body type, ages, astronomical factors, genetic determinations, and so forth, each produce a new triangle. It is the constant tension between the complexity of human dynamics and the inherent properties of a given number which gives the metasexual act its defining nature. The amount of energy available gives it its scope. This can be stated as a general principle: any metasexual act is a function of energy, personality, and geometry.

Four is a difficult number. From one angle, it is two squared. Thus, many couples attempting different numbers before having come to terms with the bisexual split, go to *four*, where they do nothing more than intensify their basic dualistic bias.

In another sense, *four* is the next two-dimensional figure after three, having one more side than a triangle. As such, it offers fifteen elementary units! As follows:

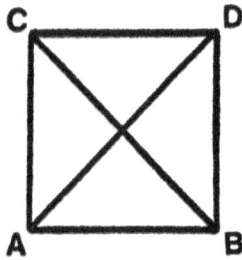

individuals: A, B, C, D; couples: AB, AC, AD, BC, BD, CD; triangles: ABC, ABD, ACD, BCD; and the overall form: ABCD. The richness of this structure is grasped when one realizes that not only are all of these sub-units operating simultaneously, but all personality components are functioning, and at the high energy level four people can generate. This gives a strong, continually changing, multi-levelled reality which only a very few are capable of experiencing and integrating.

But further, *four* is the first number which yields three dimensions.:

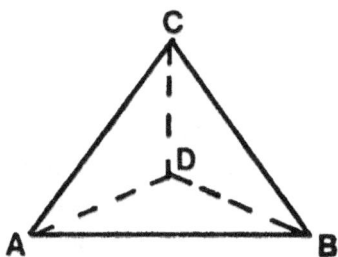

a pyramid with a triangular base. To answer the question as to what makes the difference in any given group of four between a plane with four sides and this pyramid is outside the scope of this article. But one can see that the reality of a metasexual fourth dimension, a spacetime of Einsteinian eroticism, would be the next step in this direction.

I am not personally qualified to discuss the numbers from five upward since I have not experienced them, except in gatherings of swingers who had not yet realized their metasexual nature and were piling on bodies without changing the essential consciousness of the act.

It is also fascinating to wonder at zero, or metacelibacy seen not as a renunciation, but as an embrace of, all metasex.

##

There was a time when it seemed to people that the sun revolved around the earth, a view enshrined in the Ptolemaic model of the solar system. Now, with a less parochial view, we have developed a new understanding, signalled by the introduction of the Copernican model.

The introduction of the metasexual paradigm is no less a shift in the history of our evolving understanding. The vast majority of the species has not seen past the conditioned strictures of the number *two*. And even those in the vanguard, having their orgies, still operate from the standpoint of a male-female dualism. The most sophisticated among them proclaim themselves bisexuals, not aware that this is the dead-end of that particular tunnel vision. The only way out is to go within to heal the internal split. A monad has no gender.

The question now presents itself: what form does the metasexual life style take?

I won't presume an answer. As for myself, I currently allow circumstances to guide me. Having no prejudices, no preconceptions, I am open to whatever is possible, to whoever wants to dance with me. Yet, if this is a genuine satori, as I practice the living awareness of it, a specific form may evolve. It is possible that I might one day accept a simple pattern to express my true nature: perhaps an uncomplicated heterosexual linear bond, or perhaps a gay threesome, or a life of introspective masturbation. For, if one has subsumed all forms, then one is free to manifest in any form whatsoever.

Beyond bisexuality, externals take on a different meaning than when one is caught in the male-female duality. Even the most stereotyped act is permeated with a brilliant awareness that transforms the perception of reality. To paraphrase the Zen masters:

Sucking cock,
Fucking cunt,
Empty and marvelous!

The Metasexual Manifesto

I

Metasexuality, as a concept, was first used to describe the condition of a person who had subsumed the fragmentary aspects of the erotic manifestation into a unitary appreciation. Since coining the term, however, I have come to view it rather as a category of behavior, to delineate erotic activity as such, irregardless of the consciousness of those involved. Metasexuality, properly understood, is the shadow of sexuality, a distinct modality of being not to be confused with sex per se.

Sex is, as the traditionalists have it, a vehicle for making babies, and nothing else. Sex, qua sex, is for the propogation of the species, and for no other reason. I hold this definition to be correct. However, there is a vast realm of erotic behavior which falls outside this stricture, and for that I have designated the term *metasex*.

This birfurcation in terminology, which reflects a real split in the use of our energy, requires a third term to connote the matrix which embraces both sex and metasex, and for this I employ the word *eroticum*. The eroticum is divided into two categories, sex and metasex, the distinction between which is crucial to a sane understanding of our erotic deportment.

Sex is biological; metasex is psychophysical. Sex, the biological eroticum, is for procreation and for no other reason; metasex, the psychophysical eroticum, is for any other reason whatsoever. Sex involves the continuation of the species, and is a relatively rare activity; it has to do with the entire problem of culture and civilization, and might be labelled "work eroticum". Metasex is for pleasure, for expressing affection, for exchanging energy, for money, for communication and explotation, for meditation, etc., and it might be labelled "play eroticum".

The conditions of sex are imposed by the requirements of biology; it involves a male and a female, penetration by penis into vagina, and ejaculation at the period of fertility. The conditions of metasex, on the other hand, are widely variegated, and are not concerned with the details of the act, whether it be among men and women, among men, among women, or whether it is among people who have known one another for some time or among strangers, or whether it is a function of mutual caring or done dispassionately, or whether it involves more or less than two people, or whether it is physically conventional or partakes of extreme forms.

Sex and metasex also each have a different quality of tone or texture. With sex, reverence and responsibility are the guiding attitudes; for not only the act itself is relevant, but one must be aware of the full dimension of the consequences. To create another human being is the highest act we are capable of and to engage in it lightly is, unfortunately, a malpractice of epidemic proportions. Also, through sex, one's vision extends to questions of survival, relationship, culture, education; for these are the legacies we bequeath to our children. With metasex, the necessary quality is compassion. Since the circumstances of metasex are so flexible and range over the full spectrum of human behavior, it is all the more essential that the participants do not lose sight of one another's humanity. This means that there be no exploitation, no lying, no damage.

Making proper distinctions has been called the first step in wisdom, and Confucius has stressed the importance of "rectifying the names". It soon became obvious to me that the failure to distinguish between sex and metasex lay at the very core of all our erotic difficulties, and by extension, into the trenchant problems of our civilization. *The basic error in all erotic thinking lies in muddying the aesthetic of metasex with the moral contingencies of sex, and of subverting the mystery and grandeur of sex with the relativistic values of metasex.*

Using this method of differentiation, we come upon an immediate difficulty. How are we to think and talk about the eroticum if our entire vocabulary is based on the failure to make the distinction between sex and metasex? Our terms are based on outmoded models, and we are burdened with concepts such as homosexual, bisexual, perversion, and all the lists of anatomical details. This is the result of viewing metasex from the standpoint of sexual requirements. Sexually, of course, there is only one way to do it: male and female in genital intercourse; and from that perspective the index of Krafft-Ebing makes sense. But once we see that within the metasexual purview these sub-categories are meaningless, we must find a new way to articulate our erotic experiences.

One may ask: why talk about the eroticum at all? And from an ideal aspect, we ought not to talk at all. Yet, until the time when we are all so enlightened that there is nothing more to say, sex and metasex will form a part of our discourse. To provide a vehicle for grasping and communicating erotic behavior and feeling, then, I came to the concept of *mode*, which is the paradigmatic mood within which the activity takes place. It is intended to displace all questions of detail, number, and gender, and put sex and metasex in a more fluid context.

Using this model, we will more closely approximate the reality of the erotic condition. For with the rubric of mode, sex finds its proper tone, and metasex is given its full freedom of expression. Metasexually. There is no real difference between what two men do in bed, from what three women might do in bed, nor from what a man and a woman do in bed. To label the action homosexual or bisexual or heterosexual is divisive, alienating us from one another as human beings first and foremost. The old criteria, seen in the light of the new paradigm, are primitive and wasteful. We should be adult enough to discard false standards of categorization, no matter how historically hallowed they are.

Before going into a description of the modes and of the specific quality of sexual and metasexual dynamics, I would like to put all the information constituting the model into schematic form, to use as a diagram to refer to.

THE EROTICUM

SEX Biological, "work"	METASEX Phsychophysical, "play"
A Function of Responsibility	A Function of Compassion
Reverential Mode	Procreative Mode Theatrical Mode Therapeutic Mode Romantic Mode Masturbatory Mode Zen Mode
Number: Two Type: Male and Female Activity: Penetration by penis into vagina followed by ejaculation, during a period of fertility.	Number: Any Type: Any Mixture of Gender Activity: Anything desired by the participants

This covers any possible erotic activity for any reason whatsoever, clearly distinguishes between sex and metasex, provides a new means with which to discuss and think about the erotic, and makes obsolete practically our entire "sexual" vocabulary. Through this paradigm, it is possible to arrive at a place through linguistic means which the liberation groups are attempting to reach through political means. For if we change the way we think and speak about the eroticum, the social manifestations of confusion and hostility will more easily disappear.

II

The modes of sex and metasex are my own rationalizations. I offer them as private considerations which may have universal application. I feel that if this paradigm is accepted, others will add new modes to the list, and a new erotic language be born, one which includes the mathematics of metasex.

1. The Procreative Mode: derives, or borrows, from the conditions of sex. Through it one appropriates the ambience of baby-making-sex to a form of metasexual interaction. The feelings and attitudes of sex can take place where reproduction is not the issue, between two men, for example, or between a man and a woman where birth control measures have been taken. To operate in this mode it is only necessary not to throw out the bath water with the baby. In our era of general superficiality, and under the spectre of overpopulation, the experience of procreative fucking has diminished drastically.

The most distinctive quality of this mode is a kind of urgency. By which I don't mean frenzy. There is, in the black culture, a term which captures its texture perfectly: it is called "rooting." It refers to lodging the penis deep inside the vagina and then "rooting around" as though a stick were being dug into the earth. If we remember that the word fuck derives from the idea of planting, and cunt means to hollow out, then it is clear that rooting is simply preparing the ground for the implantation of the seed. With this mode there is a quality of silence which has nothing to do with whether the participants make sounds or not. There is an almost holy intimacy which is unmistakable, an infolding, a profound taking-in that does not appear elsewhere.

Although there is no plan to produce a flesh-and-blood child, the procreative mode does allow a birth to take place, for it involves a peculiar energy bond that is highly vitalizing. Those using it give birth to an awareness which strengthens the body and exalts the soul. What is born is a vibration of goodness that is a real force in the overall evolution of the species. Those who fuck in this mode are simply made better by the experience, and to the degree that it fecundates their lives, they have brought virtue into being.

It is obvious that two men having anal intercourse, and a man and a woman in oral intercourse, for example, can experience the vibration of the procreative mode. Sexually, this is a heretical notion; but metasexually, it is part of understanding that the mythic structures through which we apprehend reality are within our power to formulate, once we know what it is that we are doing.

2. The Theatrical Mode: is a function of psychic distance, and entails the notion of performance. In this mode, there is always an audience, which may consist of actual onlookers, or may be the projected awareness of the participants viewing the act as though from the outside.

The theatrical mode requires a lightness of touch, a deftness. This refers not to the activity but to a quality of mind. The participants may be involved in something as "heavy" as flagellation, but the psychological set within which they amuse themselves must not grow ponderous. Taken literally, this mode may generate costuming and the explicit assumption of roles, e.g. virgin and debauchee, prostitute and client. It is interesting that, existentially, there is no difference between a couple's playing a game of prostitution and a person's paying a stranger to have intercourse.

The major danger of the theatrical mode is solipsism, which has a tendency to cut the circuits of energy flow between the actors and actresses. The acting-out of fantasy requires steady attention. Here the importance of compassion is clear, for it spells the difference between people's using and abusing one another. To have two or more fantasies brought to life through the eroticum without the entire affair's degenerating into confusion requires the skill of acrobats. And to maintain the "act" as an *act*, at the level of good theatre, without the admixture of psychopathy, presupposes soundness on the part of those involved.

The style may vary widely, ranging from classical through improvisatory approaches. There may be a script or the scene can begin with no more than roughly defined characters. There may be dialogue and costume, or not. Above all else, it is a *play*, both in the sense of a theatre piece and in the sense of a child-like activity. It is both sophisticated and innocent. Like dance, it sculpts contours in time and space, using only the body as a medium. One can perform either tragedy or comedy or drift deliciously into irony.

Still, this is but the literal aspect of the mode. There is another form which might be called the-theatre-as-the-real, or in eastern semantic, dharma drama. Here, there is no specific content, but only an awareness of the mode itself. The participants communicate telepathically and infuse their condition with full consciousness of the psychic structure. They take themselves to the limits of the conceptual artifact and enter the awareness of the voidness of existence. They then fuck in emptiness.

In this situation, aware of themselves as in and of the universe entire, they become the channels for all roles. They fuck archetypally, passing through the guises of gods and goddesses, demons, animals, ancient and modern races, historical entities, mythic figures, and all life forms in general. Perhaps the poetic vision which most completely evokes the theatrical mode in its total richness is that of The Dance of Shiva.

The theatrical mode ranges, then, from the literal use of theatrical props, dramatic structures, and audience, to the cosmic awareness of the universe-as-theatre. It is at once potentially the most mundane and most encompassing of all the modes.

3. The Therapeutic Mode: is the trickiest, since it simultaneously liberates repressed feelings and perpetuates the expression of those feelings. By doing the first, one makes the unconscious conscious and grows saner and healthier; by the

second, one reinforces restrictive habit patterns. The point of this mode is to allow the first while dissolving the second.

My first contact with this mode came one evening when, during a long and frenzied spell of metasex, the woman I was with burst first into sobs, then began wailing, and finally released a skin-prickling scream that shrivelled my erection. It was some years before the publication of *The Primal Scream*, so I had no handy metaphor with which to understand the phenomenon. I learned more about this mode during a period of neo-Reichian therapy, working on breaking through the body armor, the deep organic tensions which form the defense system against feeling and perception.

I started to realize that when I became, through regression, a baby reaching up for mother's embrace and breast, the motions and sounds I made—gurgling, cooing, pursing my lips, yearning with my chest—were exactly what I often did while sucking cock. Again, in the midst of reviving an old anger, as I lay on the therapeutic mattress, my fists clenched, whipping my head from side to side, shouting "no" over and over again, I saw that this was indistinguishable from expressions I made while being fucked and from expressions made by others while I fucked them.

It did not take too long to see that erotic energy was the equivalent of the therapeutic ambience, therapeutic technique, or drugs, in releasing repressed states of being. The one difference was that during metasex, one did not ordinarily link the resultant feelings with incidents and patterns of one's life. Thus, metasex could provide abreaction, but usually did not allow integration. Yet, if used consciously and correctly, it might provide the most powerful therapeutic tool at our disposal.

I suffered some ambivalence for a while, since it seemed profane to use the eroticum as a vehicle for therapy, but when I had understood the concept of mode more profoundly, the difficulty dissolved. It occured to me that this paradigm was a potent mythic structure within which to pursue greater self knowledge. For a while, fucking was not unlike going to see an analyst. I began to link certain postures with the expression of repressed states, and as that took place, my very behavior in bed underwent a transformation.

With those partners to whom I was able to explain these ideas, metasex in the therapeutic mode became an exciting and sometimes devastating activity. We could proceed openly to explore the psychosomatic ground of our personalities. There was the added advantage of dispensing with expensive, professional help. And there was an interesting side-effect: once a given manifestation, say, spanking, was seen as a need for punishment born of childhood fixation, then I became free to experience that activity *an sich*, within itself. Once the energy is generated and the etiology revealed, one is the master of the wide range of erotic forms.

Within each adult, the child lives. It is necessary to let the child come forth and be, to exercise its faculties, especially those which were distorted through negative conditioning at an early age. In the therapeutic mode, one allows these usually hidden aspects of the self to find their expression, and in so doing creates perhaps the most poignantly beautiful gestures of the body and face in the entire realm of erotic response, as well as discovers feelings which give the metasexual act a unique depth and texture.

4. The Romantic Mode: lies embedded in western historical consciousness. It is linked, inextricably, with the word "love", a concept outside the eroticum per se. To fuck with someone one is romantically in love with is undoubtedly the most exhilirating form of metasex. There is a totality, a joy, an overall sensation of rapture unparalleled in the other modes. This is the kingdom of yearning fulfilled and unfulfilled.

The basic requirement for this mode is a willingness to follow the emotions to their heights and depths. This imparts a recklessness to the romantic mode that must be reckoned with, for one becomes prone to extreme statements. The words, "I love you," or "Marry me," or "I want to be with you forever," come easily to the lips. This is a natural phenomenon, for at moments of great feeling only great declarations will satisfy.

Here the question of truth enters in. To say something so definite in a moment of passion has the ring of truth. However, when the feeling disappears, the description of that feeling, the testament to permanence, is oddly bereft of meaning. It is certainly a grand thing to mean in the morning what one has said the night before, but that need not be a precondition to saying such things. If the romantic mode is understood among the participants, then they may enjoy a lifetime of ecstasy in a single encounter, and when the encounter is finished, return to a different vibration without feeling that their words must continue to haunt them.

In this mode, one is free to wax poetic, and the effect on language can be dazzling. This is especially true for first meetings, although it can be enjoyed by old married couples. There are the classic settings: ships at sea, foreign countries, mountaintop meadows. And there is a prediliction for certain props, such as wine, marijuana, and music. Its special season is spring. Lowered lids, palpitations, rushes, languorous limbs, and fragile fucking are marks of the mode. As in everything, of course, styles may vary, in the way that Wordsworth is different from Scriabin.

The romantic mode generates such powerful feelings that there is the constant danger of its transforming, or infecting, one's life as a whole. The most extreme examples are those Japanese lovers who, forbidden to have one another, tie themselves together and hurl themselves off cliffs, to die clenched in one another's arms. Also, this kind of metasex can be so addictive that one forsakes all other modes, and becomes monomaniacal. The guiding principle of this mode is ultimate union, and thus has overtones of mysticism.

5. The Masturbatory Mode: is in many ways the home mode. Giving ourselves pleasure through touch is one of our first activities, and masturbation itself is often our introduction to eroticism. Much has been made of this form of gratification's being a substitute for "the real thing," but again, this is a sexual judgement upon a metasexual matter. Metasexually, someone choosing masturbation as a sometime or often or even total means of expression is no more or less valid than any other way of doing it.

All who have masturbated without guilt know that it can provide the most intense orgasms, clear searing explosions which take one out of the body altogether and into a different consciousness. Also, the masturbatory mode does not limit one to masturbation. Two or more people can perform the motions of fucking or sucking or stroking and have the thing be simply a more complex way of having everyone bring himself or herself off. This is a subtle and delicate game, involving responsibility for one's own cycles, yet requiring sensitivity to the inner workings of the other(s).

Behaviorally, the masturbatory mode favors the tendency to celibacy, which is the final step in auto-eroticism. Not by repression, but by progression, one learns to cycle the erotic energy totally within one's body, and thus becomes self-contained. This homeostasis is considered by some to be the highest form of erotic evolution.

6. The Zen Mode: is produced through transmodality. An act may begin in the theatrical mode and shift to the therapeutic. Or different participants may play different modes at the same time, something like a piece of music played by instruments in different keys. Dissonance is seen to be nothing other than a special form of harmony. The concept of mode is itself shaken, and finally bursts open, until the conceptual curtain lifts and all imagery dissolves. As with the Zen experience proper, there is little to say about this mode. It carries a unique sense of the moment's utter reality, and within that there lie all the joy and terror of coming face to face with The Nakedness.

III

As against my massive involvement in metasexual activity, my experience of sex has been limited. My metasexual fucking resulted in three unwanted pregnancies, but until recently I had never fucked with the intention of making a baby. Through that experience, I came upon the notions of responsibility and reverence as the basis of sexual behavior.

Sex implies morality, by which I do not mean conventional morality which, as Mr. Krishnamurti rightly points out, is immorality. I mean conscience, that quality of sensitivity which distinguishes right from wrong not on the basis of some orthodox code or preconceived ideal, but through an awareness of the nature of life in general and of humanity in particular. To use the current phrase, it is an ecological consciousness. The mode of sex, reverence, is nothing other than a profound susceptibility to all the implications of having a child. This requires shunning sentimentality on one hand and callousness on the other. To raise a child is the most difficult yoga we have, and requires that one's own life be so firmly rooted in righteousness, that one's organism be so finely attuned, that the task flows naturally from one's deepest sources, without thought. For the moment one fucks to make a baby, one asks, "And in what sort of a world will this child be born?" And then a thorough and unceasing questioning begins.

In my own situation, Lucinda, the woman with whom I planned to have a child, and I, discontinued our birth control measures, and entered the fields of sex. We first noticed a change in the priorities. Although we still experienced sensual pleasure, orgasm and the waves of excitation and release, these qualities took second place to the serious realization that we were performing the holy and awe-inspiring ritual of actually creating another human being. Puny, awkward creatures that we were, we had within us the power to bring another person to life, a person who would grow and become very much like ourselves and pick up the cycle of life where we left off. In the process of that recognition, we saw our own deaths quite clearly.

A far-reaching chain of insight coiled about us. For suddenly, issues that had seemed academic became vital. A line from Dylan came to mind: "You've hurled the worst fear/that can ever be hurled/the fear to bring children/into the world." At once, not only the species, but we as individuals, were on trial, and on all counts from the personal to the geopolitical. For example, we both smoke, and are guilty about being enslaved by a self-destructive habit. Now the question: will the nicotine we ingest into our blood streams infect the child? And more subtly: shall the child have parents who are still prey to debilitating habits?

Further, will I, knowing the extraordinary effect for ill which lurks in any implicit or explicit dishonesty about erotic feelings by parent toward child, be able to love my child physically? That is, to hold and fondle it, and accept the heavy erotic component of that behavior, and maintain what erections may come, and still not damage or limit its psyche by imposing too strong an impress while it is still young? And when it is older? What are my real feelings about incest? Do I believe it is categorically wrong?

And what of the fact that almost any school I send the child to will be a factory run by mindless conformists, processing human beings on a conveyor belt of pseudo-knowledge the way automobile parts are run through on an assembly line? What of the fact that we live in a world where only a few know even of liberty, much less freedom? And what of the realities of monstrous warfare, and unwholesome food, and foul water, and filthy air? The human species is making a concerted effort to prove conclusively that it is the lowest form of life on earth, and into such a situation, what is the purpose of bringing a child?

Such thoughts put a definite cast on the quality of our fucking. Ranging from existential speculation to ecological evaluation to character analysis, I was unable to rouse the dragon of psychophysical lust. Our sex became tentative, and on a number of occasions we did not make a sound, but coupled in stillness, as though we were listening for something other than what was going on in the two of us.

When Lucinda's first period of fertility passed, we were, by definition, returned to our metasexual playground, to our moaning and heavy breathing, to our pyrotechnics. We became, once again, a man and a woman picking their way through the erotic monkeybars of our epoch. From anal intercourse to small orgies, we continued in the annotated routines of the carnal circus. We turned to an exploration of the metasexual modes, discovering the nuances of theatrical fucking and the dynamics of the therapeutic attitude.

Then, the menses, and the realization that we had missed the first time around, and would try again. The next cycle provided a different and deeper angle of penetration into the nature of sex. One night I was on top and plowed her like a farmer burrowing in soft earth. Another night she was on top and took me fiercely, while I, sensate and inert, felt the seed sucked from my body. It seemed certain that a child conceived during one kind of fucking would be quite different from one conceived during the other. And a new element of study entered in, and we began to examine, in a way we hadn't before, what it is that we actually do when we fuck, and when we come. What thoughts do we have, what feelings? Who, in short, are we when we merge our bodies and our minds in that singular way? For, with the purpose of our fucking so clearly defined, the epiphenomenal aspects stood out in sharp light.

Concurrently, our metasexual involvements grew richer, for we no longer confused them with what we were doing sexually. One afternoon, Lucinda and I went swimming with another couple in a private stream where we could take off our clothes. Jack and Susan had had a threesome with Lucinda some months earlier, and so on this day there was the open question as to whether we would make it four. We spent a long summer day swimming, drinking wine, smoking grass, and letting time melt away, until we might have been stone age citizens on a picnic in an ancient forest. The sun beat down in its six dimensions.

I looked at Jack and Susan a long time, for I had never seen either of them naked before. The sway of Jack's cock, the curl of his shoulders, the line of his forearms, were tinglingly erotic, as were the curve of Susan's lower back, the high arch of her feet, the smoky directness in her eyes. But within five minutes, I felt my attention wander. It was not that they were not attractive enough to spend more time on, but that my senses and sight and thought had been sated, while my other senses had been starved. I had not touched, smelled, tasted, or listened to them in all that time. Nor had our minds merged. We were definitely on the threshold of the eroticum, but there seemed to be no way to cross over into it.

I considered the situation more fully, and saw that I had, out of habit, fallen into the old trap of evaluating the quartet in sexual categories: two men, two women, two pairs of bonded couples, homosexual-heterosexual-bisexual combinations, and all the conceptual paraphenalia which is not relevant to the metasexual realm. But as soon as I translated the situation into energy terms, and saw that the problem was simply one of sensory deprivation, the block to further flow dissolved. We were not allowing ourselves full sensory communication with one another.

I mused on the fact that our erotic lives are often so strained because we do not, in our day to day living, experience one another with more than our eyes and our ears. I can't count the number of men and women I have been to bed with only to discover that I had wanted little more than to touch or taste or smell a part of them, much in the way that two dogs will greet one another with sniffs and licks. This problem has ramifications outside of the eroticum, but it is the eroticum which is most crucially affected. Without full sensory freedom, metasex is stilted and sex is improverished.

If we lived in a civilization where we did not operate like automatons, our sexual activities would lose their vulgarity and our metasexual encounters would shed their air of preciosity. If I can smell a woman's cunt, I may not have to fuck her. But if I have to fuck her just to get to smell her cunt, the erotic act is demeaned. Actually, one might define the eroticum as that which occurs when people have had their sensual fill of one another, and find an energy which at once subsumes and transcends all the senses.

At the swimming hole, able to sluff off the murkiness born of faulty designation, I found the vibration of the atmosphere changing. There was no question of whether or not we would have sex, but rather, would we be able to find a mode within which to enjoy a bit of metasexual play? Metasex, involving perception, sensation, emotion, thought, instinctual movement, and muscular coordination, is a unitary activity. And as so often happens, once I saw that, the mood relaxed. We swam together, and afterwards ended by sitting in a circle on the grass. I looked at the people around me and let my hands find their own impulse. I touched Susan's breasts, Jack's thighs, Luanda's mouth. The touch was simple information gathering, the satisfaction of tactile curiosity. From there, the rhythm began. We started to caress one another, to smell each other's bodies, to lick one another's skin. Subtly, a change came over us, and without any formal announcement, we sank into the sweet embrace of metasex.

The rest of the afternoon brought about the standard developments: the fucking and sucking, the fingering and stroking, the clutching and writhing. At such moments it is irrelevant who does what to whom or how. And to classify what we did as an orgy is to lapse into stale terminology. We gave ourselves sensory freedom, and from that release flowed warmth, joy, excitement, and pleasure. In such a circumstance, it was of no importance whether I held a cock in my mouth or a cunt in my hand, whether the penetration into my anus was Jack's cock or Susan's finger.

In a few weeks, Lucina and I continued our attempts at pregnancy, and discovered deeper changes. Since the ejaculation of sperm is intended for procreation, then when insemination is not the issue, ejaculation is superfluous. I came to the conclusion logically, but it also operated spontaneously within me. More and more often during her non-fertile periods, we fucked without my ejaculating. It was the entrance into maithuna, or tantra, or Taoist yoga. And it produced in astonishing revelation: that I, as a man, could have many orgasms which had nothing to do with the shooting off of sperm. I found that I could come emotionally, or psychically, or through a peaking of sensation, or as a result of a sympathetic vibration with her. For years I had envied women the capacity for multiple orgasm, but was blind to that ability within myself (except when being fucked myself and experiencing anal and oral climaxes) because I was confusing the sexual orgasm, which indeed does require ejaculation, with the metasexual orgasm, in which ejaculation is not a necessary component.

IV

Given all this, we find that nothing changes. Everyone will continue to do what he or she pleases, or is driven to. The only claim for this paradigm is that it will remove all confusion as to what precisely what one is doing in the eroticum. To give one example, the problem of jealousy is so difficult to deal with because we don't distinguish between real possessiveness and neurotic clinging. Between a man and a woman having sex, that is, trying to have a child, jealousy is a natural feeling, evolved in our animal nature. Between those having metasex, however, to be jealous is to be immature. Knowing that as a fact is the first step toward dealing intelligently with the syndrome.

We will go on, as a species, playing out whatever script we write for ourselves, within the bounds enforced by our limitations as creatures. There will be men who prefer men, women who prefer woman, men and women who prefer the opposite gender; there will be threesomes and wife-swapping and orgies; there will be flagellations and people being pissed on in public urinals; there will be tender hand holding and forceful fist-fucking. But within this new model of sex and metasex, we may make peace with our proclivities. Those who take it upon themselves to propogate the species will do one thing; the rest are free to choose their own form.

Ultimately, we may rid ourselves of false notions of perversion. *Sexually, the only perversion is to fuck without reverence and responsibility; metasexually, the only perversion is to fuck without compassion.*

As of this writing, the child has not been conceived. But if it is, I find it imperative that it be born in a world where the problems of sex, the ancient stumbling block of Adam and Eve, be perfectly distinguished from metasex, a rather different aspect of the human condition. To accomplish this, more is required than scientific research, although the work of people like Kinsey, Johnson, and Masters, is of immense value; and it requires more than political activism, although the liberation groups have performed an indispensible service; it requires more than pornographic liberty, although that has helped expose the fantasies of a nation.

Beyond all that, it is necessary that we understand, that we *grasp*, the very nature of the division between sex and metasex, that we change the language we use to talk and think about the eroticum, that we realize the implications of this new paradigm for every facet of our behavior, going from marriage through promiscuity, from puritanism to debauchery, from chauvinism to real affection.

Then we might have sex which is austere and grand, and metasex which is as beautiful as a rainbow. And we might begin to sort out the murky legacy of lust which is such a large part of our heritage, and turn our faces toward honesty, survival, and true human dignity.

Many Are Chosen but Few Spend the Night

A Working Model of Promiscuity

After my recent divorce, I entered a period of sport-fucking, that already well-documented effort to burn out all traces of the previous partner and re-establish one's identity as an autonomous being. But within two months, the fever passed, and my delirium subsided into the dull ache and phantom-limb phenomenon reported by amputees. It was as though in losing my wife I had lost an arm, but was now learning to live without it.

When the flurry of heated exchanges died down and the bedsheets were returned from the laundry, I found myself settled into a pattern which contained all the drawbacks of marriage and none of its advantages. One of my many ladies had installed herself as a personality in my life and assumed the role with savage tenacity. Another woman was struggling for fiancee status. And my male lover wanted me to spend a summer with him in the country. This left little time for my work, solitude, or erotic explorations outside this self-appointed triad.

Since I was not a candidate for celibacy and did not yet want to marry again, I was forced to examine my condition with an eye to defining some kind of new order against the tension of conflicting demands. My therapist's injunction to "feel" the reality took me only so far; it became necessary to erect a new conceptual framework to serve as a map, or guiding principle, for what would otherwise remain a mere interface space between marriage and celibacy.

Behaviorally, I was promiscuous. But that word is drenched with such negative connotations, conjuring images of one-night stands, single's bars, indiscriminate and evasive couplings, that I was loathe to apply it to myself. Yet a word is the property of all, and I was impelled to rescue this one from the miasma of imprecise and prejorative meanings which have enveloped it, and to infuse it with fresh life.

The common cultural judgement on the state gives it at best a transitional status, a rather low-grade condition appearing before or between marriages; it is seen as something for the young, the immature, or the immoral. Conversely, it is secretly admired as a kind of paradisical lifestyle, offering the excitement of chase, conquest, and a progression of new bodies. The myths of the *Playboy* pad and the *Cosmopolitan* cunt are as viable for one large segment of the population as the special divinity of Jesus is for another.

The first step in my re-evaluation of promiscuity lay in understanding that it is neither the edge of erotic revolution or an erotic garbage dump, but rather a model of feeling and behavior which stands alongside of marriage and celibacy as a means of dealing with the endless conflict between fucking and the rest of human activity. It is no more or less than *one of three valid paths available for understanding, ordering, and predicting change and recurrence in the movements of erotic energy.* This means accepting that the state has its own structures, laws, etiquette, pleasures, sorrows, and stretches of boredom. Re-defining promiscuity involves a conceptual adjustment, a change in basic vibration, and a radical metamorphosis of inner identity. As I was later to learn, it also entails a terrible austerity, the wielding of an erotic Occam's razor which requires the compassionate cruelty of a surgeon's scalpel.

The second step concerned meeting people who are themselves promiscuous, that is, who had attained the awareness I was just learning to articulate. This is difficult, for most women are so heavily conditioned toward marriage that their whole lives are often movements toward or away from that situation. More than a few I encountered exhibited the most reckless pregnancy need, unconsciously acting out old courtship scenarios, treating fucking as a favor women bestowed upon men. Another type retained the rhetoric of enlightened promiscuity but were merely alienated, incapable of dimensional relating.

Men posed a parallel problem. From a metasexual viewpoint, of course, the gender of the partner one chooses is not germane to any serious erotic consideration, and terms like bisexuality are too stiff and divisive to be of much use. Most men, such as I might meet in bars or at the baths, want no more than a brief fling, and fucking with them is pretty much like a wrestling match. Here, again, promiscuity is taken in its debased sense. Also, the marriage syndrome is quite strong beneath the surface manifestations, and so-called promiscuous behavior is often merely a false veneer covering a deep need for bonding.

After aligning my internal awareness with the condition of those I related to, I was able to discern the basic principle of the promiscuity paradigm. In celibacy, the primary relationship is to the *self*; in marriage, it is to the *other*. In promiscuity, the primary relationship is to the concept. Promiscuity, in a Duchampsian sense, can be considered "conceptual eroticism." In it, we serve one another as vehicles for the most perfect expression of erotic energy. As the celibate is committed to self-development, and the married undertakes the task of perpetuating the species, the promiscuate tends the flame of pure Erotic Idea.

The danger here lies in using the notion to rationalize an intrinsic dehumanization of erotic relationships. To avoid this, an extraordinary honesty, with oneself and with one's partners, is essential. If the relationships are themselves warm, tender, and compassionate, it does not matter that the metaphor which governs them is cold. Romanticism is no longer our reigning myth, and models drawn from cybernetics are clearly the thought-shapes of the future present. Even in the esoteric wing of human knowledge, the Gurdjieffian machine analogy provides the most compelling current of the century. Accepting a new model of promiscuity involves a new understanding of what it is to be human. This may be used, as many ideas have been used, as an instrument of perversity; but as with all human activity, the final arbiter is the individual conscience.

After coming to terms with general considerations, I began to chart the actual flow of my specific promiscuous evolution, and was able to draw the following diagram:

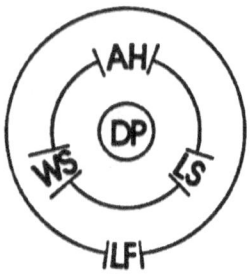

At the center is the Defining Principle. The first circle contains a Wife Surrogate (WS), a Lover Surrogate (LS), and an Ad Hoc situation (AH). The outer circle holds a Lover-Friend (LF).

The Wife Surrogate is a woman with whom I have developed a steady relationship, reciprocal at all levels. The Lover Surrogate is a man with whom I share traditional romantic values, our energies going from chest to chest more than from genital to genital. The Ad Hoc situation is an open space, variously filled by vagrant episodes, occasional threesomes, and so forth. The Lover Friend is an ex-wife who I see a few times a year and with whom I always share good talk and warm fucking.

The single most important fact about these relationships is that they are structural rather than personal. They remain unchanged in texture, activity, and feeling no matter who happens to be occupying the space at any given time. Should the Wife Surrogate leave, the next woman to take that position would, from the very first day, assume the depth, complexity, and quality of that role, and continue in that fashion for so long as we maintained the contract. To define the rule: for the promiscuate, all individuals are unique, and no one uniqueness is given special prominence over any other.

With the passage of time, the diagram changed its form periodically. For a while it contained a Peripheral Woman (PW) who called me once or twice a week and with whom I slept once or twice a month. But I found the presence of that category too draining on my energy and deleted it. Of course, this description has both a universal and specific aspect. Anyone entering the state of promiscuity seriously will develop a structure like this, but the details will vary from person to person.

Once I was able to be clear about my condition, I could explain to each of the people in my life precisely where they fit in relation to myself and to one another. Some found the notion grotesque, and wanted no more to do with me. But more than a few, both inside and outside the circle, were grateful for the clarity. I was able to distinguish the true promiscuates from the closet celibates and secret seekers after marriage on the basis of which grasped the necessity for such a conceptual structure. The motto became, *No Passion Without Paradigm.*

Too often we have taken the magic, mystery, and power of the erotic spell for granted. Fucking, the source of life and perhaps its most complete activity, is also our most comprehensive metaphor. Erotic energy is very pure, very fine, and comparable to the energy one develops while doing zazen or other meditational practices. In the act of fucking we pierce one another's flesh with flesh, breathe one another's breath, drink one another's fluids, swim in one another's souls, communing telepathically on all levels, tossed upon the same billowing waves of cosmic creation and thrust into the same intergalactic calms, speaking, weeping, smiling, listening to the cries and sighs of ecstasy which punctuate the profound silence of the erotic mood. It is unquestionably grand, a gift from the gods as well as a legacy from the animals. The major insight of the promiscuate, paradoxically, is that there is no such thing as a casual fuck.

Simply because this vortex is so magnetic, it shines out of all proportion over the drab routines of our grey civilization, and we seem unable to deal with it sensibly. Celibacy, ideally, is the awareness of the splendor of eros, a decision to treat that ground as so sacred one will not walk upon it. But all too often it is practiced out of fear of opening oneself, or out of some misplaced notion of holiness. Marriage can be a pact between two people who find fucking so special they decide never to share it with anyone else. Or else it may become a clutching jealousy which ultimately smothers the erotic spark. Promiscuity also has two faces: one sees fucking as a sublime activity, its own raison d'etre, and structures human relationship as a vehicle of erotic worship; the other continually cheapens the erotic impulse by pretending that it has no meaning, seeing fucking merely as a way of scratching an itch.

The exalted view of promiscuity, however, for all its lyrical charm, contains its own problems. The marriage reflex is the most trenchant, and it insidiously reappears whenever I feel it has been extirpated. Allied to this is the entire area of conflicting demands on my time and energy, a difficulty which prompted the notion of setting up a pecking order. Then there is the question of dumping. How does one tell one's Wife Surrogate that she has been cycled out and replaced by yesterday's Ad Hoc adventure? Specialization is perhaps the most thorny issue. Does one define the totality of one's erotic life in terms of the full range of people with whom one is involved, responding in part to each; or does one seek full expression with each every time?

I have found no definitive answers yet. The bonding reflex, on the level of social conditioning, may be dealt with consciously; but as a biological mechanism it is intransigent. The pecking order situation may be eased by having the various individuals in the circles meet and come to an understanding in relation to excessive demands. The problem of termination is eased since each of the people I see has his or her own erotic web. Breaking off with someone doesn't exile that person to isolation, but simply occasions an alternation of his or her own erotic structure. Also, anyone in the inner circle can move into the second circle, not an uncomfortable location. The question of specialization, very subtle and complex, requires much more experience and analysis before I can define its elements.

These and related difficulties indicate that the state of promiscuity presents a range of challenges as wide and deep as provided by marriage or celibacy. Those I have indicated represent first impressions, and I imagine that anyone entering this realm will find his or her own angles on the situation. My purpose in presenting, however sketchily, my current structure is to give an example of the model. My major concern lies in indicating that promiscuity offers a sane, adult, and compassionate alternative to marriage and celibacy, and one which requires research, self-awareness, strength, and a daring leap into a new realization of one's erotic makeup.

Beyond this, once promiscuity is given its proper respect, there is the possibility of movement from one state to another with greater ease. The end of a marriage need not mean a leap into degradation or loneliness, but merely a sidestep into a different mode. Hybrid forms are possible. One gay couple I know has been together for five years, and since the first year they have not fucked one another, but maintained all erotic liaisons outside their relationship. Thus they have the emotional and psychological security of marriage, the austerity of mutual celibacy, and the erotic flexibility of promiscuity, all within a single life style.

From my own experience, I feel it is essential that the promiscuate be widely understood as a separate and legitimate type, on a par with the married and the celibate. Such a person blends the solitary quality of celibacy with the bonding capacity of marriage, adding a third and unique ingredient, conceptual primacy. Up until now, promiscuity has been treated by society, by psychological opinion, and by its practitioners, as some form of aberration, or else as a fantasy fulfillment. Promiscuates fell into the mindless habit of fucking first and asking questions later, coming to despise themselves for qualities which seemed debased only because they were not being totally expressed, poisoning themselves with an unconscious wistful hankering for marriage or a secret idea that celibacy was the superior way.

Once promiscuity is taken seriously, foolish and degrading behavior will be seen for what it is and one will have a much more difficult time justifying one's weakness and neurosis. Promiscuity is diametrically opposed to trashing, and perhaps the major reason why it has not been accepted as a viable lifestyle is that such an understanding might seal off an escape route for millions who have few other ways to deal with excessive levels of anxiety.

For myself, this is the conclusion of my current phase of exploration. A year from now, I may be married again, or celibate, or have worked out a new synthesis. But for now, while I am promiscuous, I have no choice but to understand the nature of the condition and to define it in the most rigorous terms. To be at once a person, an individual, operating within finite parameters of human relationship, and a transpersonal manifestation of pure energy, a reflection of the primal mystery of being, a living coordinate on the grid of creation, to be the actual embodiment of the principle of both/and, to have solved the problem of duality in the acid bath of eros, this is the promise held out by the path of enlightened promiscuity.

The Split Splits

Although, as Reich observed, we may begin to develop characterological tensions from as early as three weeks of age, it usually isn't until we are from between three and seven years old that our essential malformation installs itself at crucial junctures in our psychophysical infrastructure. The child undergoes incremental increases of muscular tensions, breath suppression, and perceptual distortion until some single incident activates an autonomous armor system which has no function except the maintenance of its own defenses. We can see this in nations as easily as in individuals.

This process of conditioned pathology has been variously described. In our attempt to understand why we are imperfectly made, we have evolved a full spectrum of rationalization. "Original sin" is no more or less explanatory than "cosmic ignorance" or "the emotional plague." And thousands of religions, therapies, schools of meditation, and political movements have been launched to delineate the causes of our stupidity as a species and to cure our disease.

Most recently, Janov's concept of a *primal split* has provided a useful handle for grabbing on to the problem. I remember an event which may very well have been the central factor in deciding the contours and content of my erotic life, and in providing me with a highly personal yoga through which to bring myself back into touch with myself.

I was eight years old. My mother and a neighbor woman were going shopping, and left the neighbor's two-year-old daughter with me to watch for a few minutes. My instructions were simply to see that she didn't get into mischief or hurt herself.

But the moment they left, I was filled with a deep throbbing which began in my chest and spread into my legs, until my whole body was trembling as though with cold. The little girl was lying on the floor, staring vacantly at the ceiling. My desire was strong and clear, guided by a biological genius that had not as yet been permanently deranged. Desire unstrung me, although I knew that what I was being drawn to do would be considered an act which merited severe punishment.

But with what fiendish cunning, at such an early age, I pieced together the understanding that since the girl was too young to speak, she could not report on anything I might do with her! While I couldn't articulate it as such, the relationship between truth and language stood forth in all its enticing complexity.

I had no notion of harming the child; quite the contrary, my impulses were expansive and benign, even though selfishly motivated. With untutored instinct I grasped the principle of give-to-get that it took Masters and Johnson a laboratory and a hundred exhibitionists to demonstrate. The little girl turned me on, and I wanted to make her feel good so she would make me feel good.

Taking the burden of responsibility for my need, I pulled the diaper down to her ankles. For a long while I gazed at the unformed cleft, knowing at once that any other notions of God would, for a large portion of my life, take second place to the mesmerizing appeal of that hole, I lay down next to her, unbuttoned my pants, and assumed my career as an erotic entity. I pressed my tiny penis against her crotch and rubbed myself on her, gently at first, and soon with mounting excitement.

I became lost in the mild frenzy of the act, yet I remember that the girl was relaxed and smiling throughout, and seemed to be enjoying herself in that vague way of infants. We were sharing a primitive communion and I was taken with the revelation that this simple play was the nicest thing I'd ever done with anyone. The mutual exposure games I had encountered with girls my age had always been tinged with a tingling sense of naughtiness that at once added to their intensity and eroded their naturalness. Much later in life I was to realize that what our culture considers eroticism is really a more or less sophisticated resistance to the acceptance of the flow of pleasure.

I was in the middle of a pretty good soft-cock-without-penetration fuck when I heard the front door open. I'm sure that no knock by police agents in the dead of night has even been as terrifying to anyone as that entrance was to me. It was my mother and her friend returning. My breath froze, the diaphragmatic paralysis which signals all psychic and emotional pathology. I pictured them descending on me, their faces horrible masks of anger, their curved fingers ready to tear at my eyes.

That what I was doing, in itself harmless and pleasant, a bit of natural behavior which in a sane society would evoke nothing more than an indulgent smile, would be judged a crime by the world I lived in, now represented by these mothers, is a wedge of knowledge that must have entered me through a thousand informal channels during my childhood. Without an explicit word ever having been spoken to me, I had introjected the judgment of civilization on the body.

I put my penis back and with fumbling fingers yanked the diaper back over the girl's legs. The suave lover of a few seconds earlier had rapidly disintegrated into a guilt-ridden, twitching bundle of insecurity. Perhaps if, at that instant, I had maintained myself bravely and continued in the authority of my innocence, I might have been physically beaten but would have retained my integrity. But I was a cowardly, intellectual youngster, and I capitulated without a contest.

The child, sensing the sudden tension, began to cry. And I was barely able to sit on the floor next to her and pretend to be trying to quiet her before the two women walked into the room.

The girl's mother merely picked her up and asked, "Has she been crying long?"

"No," I answered truthfully, "she just started," relieved because I had long since understood that the best way to hide a dangerous truth was with an irrelevant one.

But when I looked up at my mother, my stomach dropped, and my breathing became rapid and shallow. Her face seemed demonic in its aspect. I was convinced that she knew what I had been doing and was refraining from punishing me only to protect the family honor in front of the neighbor. In retrospect, of course, I see that I was projecting, transforming my fear into her anger so that I might suffer punishment for what I had now to accept as a sin. Also, I was still prone to the common childhood practice of imbuing one's parents with omniscience.

However, I didn't have all these fancy insights at my disposal just then, I simply shrank away from her, and a great chasm of shame opened between us. It was a space I could not bridge, for it was unthinkable that I speak my heart and mind at that moment. In that instant, our closeness ended, not to be re-established for thirty years. My Mother had become Other. And within me, the shadow self was born.

No one who has relived such experiences will be surprised at how clearly my consciousness recorded the birth of the dissembling "I." It is only with subsequent covering-over that we lose the sharpness with which we saw ourselves split ourselves in two. I understood totally, in that clarity of childhood, that the person I was—the one who found no wrong in playing with and fondling that little girl—would always be a criminal in the eyes of a world that despised both its animal and angel natures. I suffered the same understanding several years later, when I had my first erotic encounter with one of the boys in the neighborhood. But by that time I had already learned to shift the stage scenery of my psyche so that I remained protected from the pain of loss.

My life settled into a pattern that might be described as a spastic sine wave. I alternated periods of stunning hypocrisy with outbursts of introspection and physical revolt. My cycles of construction involved gluing together an image acceptable to some portion of the world; my cycles of destruction produced Shivaite dances which burned the constraining hulk of social identity. The good little boy and the unconditioned monkey chased one another around the hyperbole.

I considered this my personal aberration until I realized that this inane fluctuation represented a parody of the essential life rhythm, an infantile melodrama that constituted the core of what we have been pleased to call civilization.

In attempting to find my true place amidst the confusion, I

travelled through the classic dialectic described in Zen literature as, "Before I attained enlightenment, mountains were merely mountains; while I searched for enlightenment, mountains were no longer mountains; after enlightenment, mountains were once again mountains."

In the beginning existed the pure polymorphous perverse eroticism of the infant. When this was thwarted and mangled, and I found myself in a land of greyness and sterility, I began a long trek through the lengthy lists of variations on the theme of fragmentary fucking. Like a mystic searching for the Absolute, I yearned for the unsought and uncomplicated joy of baby delight. In the process I experienced and catalogued the entire range of erotic expression, sensation, and insight possible to a human being at the level of search.

But after the vegetative orgasms and orgy raptures, after the swoonings into conceptual sensuality, after the romance of domination and submission, after the surprisingly innocuous and often ludicrous prowlings through what have traditionally been considered the perversions, I found that only one thing had been accomplished: *I had come full circle around the wheel of human erotic experience in our time.*

Beneath all that lay the unaltered ground of my original nature. And my task was nothing other than to walk that ground, now as an adult, with simplicity, affection, and true intelligence.

But this left me precisely where I ought to have been all along and, indeed, in exactly the same situation which faces every other human being on the planet, from celibate sages to transsexual coprophiliacs.

The entire spectrum of erotic play was open to me, yet that solved nothing. I still needed to find out which way was home.

To infuse the particulars of everyday life with a sense of wonder, or to seek new forms . . . to see mystery in the obvious textures of our epochal myths, or to opt for an idiosyncratic existentialism . . . to know the infinite through the limitations of morality, or to woo transcendence . . . to enter eternity by the gateway of esoteric normality, or to become an illusion . . . these are the cunt-and-asshole, the cock-and-mouth of the smirking and caressing void.

Last week I was invited to serve as the metasexual conduit and catalyst for a fifteen-person extended family. Simultaneously, I was continuing a lengthy exploration of the meaning of monogamy.

Can the split be healed through choice, which involves denial, or shall I let myself be called by the beckoning voices into separate universes, so that, when the carcass has ceased from dreaming and the bones no longer hold together, it will be seen that from the very beginning, I have not been here at all?

About the Author

MARCO VASSI was, without a doubt, the foremost erotic writer of our generation. Praised by Norman Malier, Kate Millett, Saul Bellow, and Gore Vidal, he was not only the ultimate sexual explorer, but a literary craftsman whose own life experiences became the stuff of his fiction—expanded, of course, by a grand imagination and a full sense of the absurd.

Tragically, Vassi died from pneumonia after he had contracted AIDS.

OPEN ROAD
INTEGRATED MEDIA

Open Road Integrated Media is a digital publisher and multimedia content company. Open Road creates connections between authors and their audiences by marketing its ebooks through a new proprietary online platform, which uses premium video content and social media.